The Prodigal Son

William's Choice

Matthew J Krengel

ISBN-10:147749930x
ISBN-13:978177499306

DEDICATION

For my son and daughter, in hopes that they will enjoy reading all of their lives.

CONTENTS

I like the story because there was action when the thieves were after William and the villagers.

Taylor - 11

This book is action packed but has a good balance of Bible too.

Caden - 9

I want to read this book.

Katrina - 7

A fun story with a good message, enjoyable for all ages.

Matt - 38

ACKNOWLEDGMENTS

Thanks to my mom and my wife who have both supported me through the effort to finish this new endeavor. Also to Tim Bowden for the great cover art and Raymond Lauer for the interior art.

In a Land similar to England,
In a time like that of the Crusades,
In a house dedicated to the Savior,
Lives a boy.

Prologue

Two men sat looking down at the small village nestled in a shallow area between two hills. The first wore an assortment of leather armor and bits of chain armor, while the second wore a matched set of chain mail. Despite the ragged condition of their clothes and armor, the weapons that they held were well oiled and sharpened. They were the weapons of men who sold their swords to the highest bidder for a living. Thieves and cutthroats, they were men without honor.

"We take them when the moon is full," the second muttered. He used his sword to point to the chapel and smithy. "Make sure that the smithy and church are not burned. I don't want to have an incident like last time when someone throws a torch into the wrong window."

The other man nodded and looked darkly back at the two score ruffians crouched in the tall grasses behind the hill. They waited, eager for the chance to pillage the quiet village and take what they could. This was how they chose to live their lives, sweeping out of the vast untamed wilderness of the Wilds and looting what they could. When they had all they could carry they would disappear back into the Wilds.

"What of the lord who rode into the village and his guards?"

The leader of the bandits pondered for a moment before answering, "Kill the guards and take the noble for ransom."

"I bet he is worth a pretty pile of coins to someone in this miserable land," the first laughed.

They crept back to the waiting thieves and repeated the orders given earlier. The smaller homes outside the inner circle of dwellings could be fired immediately chances of finding something valuable inside those dwellings was slim.

"Remember, don't fire the chapel or

the smithy," the leader repeated. He frowned and the scar on his face deepened the angry look until it seemed his entire face would split. The scar on his face was a remnant of a battle long gone but it served him well now when keeping the others in line. He wore the scar proudly and used it to his advantage whenever possible.

"We understand, Scar Face." Some of the men replied as they shuffled nervously. None dared look at him in the face as they spoke, most kept their eyes averted.

"Well, someone didn't last time and we lost a good bit of plunder because of it," Scar Face reminded them. "Come on, the moon is getting ready to rise."

There was a whisper of blades leaving sheathes and the forty thieves slipped up the hill and spread out as they started down towards the sleeping village.

Duke Edward was a tall man with strapping shoulders and a thick shock of black hair cropped short. His blue eyes narrowed as he looked out the window and caught a glimmer of movement on the hill leading down to the small village. He motioned for Bernard to walk over to where he was standing and pointed to where he had seen the movement. They stood side by side inside the upper room of the only inn in the small village and looked out across the quiet collection of houses. He dropped his hand to the sword at his side and looked out across the nearby hillside as the moon rose into the sky over the northern countryside of the land of Britoria.

"Do you see something moving out there?" the Duke asked. His voice was deep and powerful, almost like a wave of rolling thunder. He turned to look at Bernard, his oldest and the most battle hardened of his men. He was fellow soldier through the Second Crusade and a powerfully built man with forty-five years behind him. Still, at his age, he was quick on his feet and his eyes missed nothing.

Bernard squinted as he looked over the hillside. "Thieves?" It took him a moment to pick out the first of the figures that was slinking down the hillside but soon he saw many more approaching. A glimmer entered his eyes as he thought of what was sure to be a pitched battle against the group of cutthroats.

"I don't see any other reason for a large group of men to be trying to approach a village at night. Not creeping like a nest of snakes," the Duke said. He picked up his long bow and motioned to the four men that had made the trip with him. The village was a stopover on their way to the City of the King; it was a yearly trip that the Duke made to secure items for trade.

"Shall we raise the warning?"

"I think we will turn the surprise on them," the Duke said with a short laugh. He was normally a solemn man and not given to laughter except on rare occasions. "Gather your bows."

Bernard and the four others grabbed the weapons and walked to the back of the inn where they were staying. They slipped out the door and headed across the hard packed dirt like men with a serious mission fixed in their minds. The man cleaning the stable gave them a startled look and glanced about nervously at the grim faces. All of the Duke's soldiers were veterans of the Second Crusade and they were as battle hardened as any man in the King's army.

"Go quietly and warn the village folk that thieves are approaching," the Duke said as he raised his hand to his lips.

The man glanced at him and nodded, his eyes grew wide. He carefully set his hay fork against the wall of the stable and vanished into the inn to wake the master of the inn.

The Duke led his men out the back of the inn and north out of the village until they were well behind the ruffians. Then they turned and ran silently around the edge of the line of thieves. When the Duke thought they had moved far enough they turned and watched. At the bottom of the hill a pair of torches suddenly flared to life and the Duke motioned to Bernard.

"Let them fire one building," the Duke muttered. He hated to risk the lives of the villagers but they could not fire into the dark blindly. Doing so would put even more of the innocent at risk. With a roaring blaze going the thieves would be easy to spot and easier to shoot. After a moment the first torch arched into the air and came to a rest on the thatched roof. The flames caught immediately on the bundles of dry straw and a few minutes later the startled scream of a woman filled the night air. Moments later a pair of panicked villagers rushed from the cottage and ran for the small well in the middle of the village.

"Fire on them," Duke Edward said as he motioned to the rest of his men. He chose an arrow from his own quiver and drew back his bow waiting to choose his target.

"Consider it done," Bernard said with a grim smile. He drew his bow back and sighted along the shaft. He aimed just below the torch and as his eyes caught the brief reflection of the fire on the steel of a weapon he released the shaft.

The Duke nodded when a startled yelp erupted from the line of dark figures. Next to him the rest of the men were lining up their own targets and the nearly invisible shafts flashed against the light of the blaze. The night was filled with panicked shouts and cries as the Duke and his guard raked the thieves and turned the ambush into a trap. Within moments half of the thieves were down on the ground calling out for mercy and help, while the others fled into the night. With their bows still held ready, the Duke led his men down off the hill and into the edge of the village.

"Sir, look out!" shouted Bernard. A tall man with a horrible scar on his face was crouched in the shadows of a building as they approached the village. He held a gleaming steel sword and leapt from where he stood swinging it at Duke Edward.

The Duke stumbled back as a wickedly sharp sword flashed where he had just been standing and Bernard drew his own blade. The fight was viscous but the outcome was decided from the moment it began. The scarred thief fought wildly and hard but he was no match for the trained soldier. Bernard worked his sword in a display of defensive prowess and when Scar Face was exhausted, Bernard knocked the sword from his adversaries hand and tripped him to the ground.

"Shall I kill him, sire?" Bernard asked? He placed his sword on the man's neck and locked his eyes on the thief. There was no compassion in the eyes of the hardened soldier, not for thieves who came only to kill and destroy what others worked hard to build.

"No," the Duke sighed. "We will not kill in cold blood, he is defeated. We will let the local magistrate of the crown deal with his fate."

"Bah, you're better off killing me,"

Scare Face growled as he spat at the Duke and was rewarded with a sharp blow across the face.

Bernard drew his sword back and as Scar Face's eyes closed for the killing blow, he snapped out a powerful kick that connected with the man's jaw. Scar Face's head snapped back and his eyes immediately glazed over.

"I am sorry sire," Bernard apologized. "I should have seen sooner that he meant to spit at you."

The Duke waved off the apology, "It is nothing, his aim was as bad as his smell and his planning." He took a handful of grass and brushed the wad of spit free of his tunic. "Now, let us see to the restraint of the remaining criminals and send a message to the king's magistrate. I am sure the dungeon at Hardarva's Wall has some free cells for them."

His men nodded and spread out as they gathered the dropped weapons and took pieces of rope offered by a villager. Quickly and efficiently they began tying the wounded men so that they could not flee. Once they were restrained, their wounds were tended despite the dark looks of the villagers.

"You won't stop me."

The Duke looked back in surprise as the thief with the horrible scar struggled against his bonds. It was amazing that he had recovered from the kick so quickly and the Duke wondered if there was more to this bandit then most men.

"I will find you and make you pay for spoiling my plans."

"Watch your tone thief," Bernard said. With a lightning fast move he snapped a right fist into the man's jaw again and once more his eyes glazed over. This time he added a gag to the ropes holding the leader of the thieves and tied it tightly into place.

"Haul them into the center of the village and tend the wounds of those that our arrows took," the Duke ordered. There were five of the thieves who were not moving at all and he pointed to the men. "Prepare them for a proper burial, those men are answering to a power higher then the king and eternity waits for them."

"Probably an eternity of fire," Bernard muttered as he hoisted one of the bodies to his shoulder.

"Yes, but we cannot know that for sure," the Duke said. "It may be that at some point in the past they trusted in the work of the Savior. That is for the One who spoke the universe into being to judge."

His men nodded and set to work, he knew not all believed as he and Bernard did but they were all loyal men and skilled soldiers.

1 – Picking Rocks

"Keep your guard up."

William grunted as he tried to lift his tired arm back into the air. The tip of his wooden practice sword rose into the air a moment too late. He cringed as he saw the sword approaching him and knew he could not stop it.

"Ouch," William grunted as his brother's wooden sword poked him in the chest.

"I told you to keep your guard up," Conrad said with an evil smile that only an older brother could muster. He swung his sword again but this time William's blade managed to intercept it. The wooden blades made loud ticking sounds as they bounced off each other.

William glared at his brother as he took a step back and tried to catch his breath. With three years separating them the battles were hardly fair, but their father insisted that they learn to defend themselves. He brushed his blond hair back from his face and launched a savage attack with his wooden stick that failed to accomplish anything. Soon his sword began to dip as his arm started to ache once again.

"Now you're just angry and wasting your energy," Bernard called from the side of the practice yard.

William's blue eyes flashed over to where the captain of the small contingent of hired soldiers sat calmly watching their mock duel. The dark-haired man shook his head and then leaned forward again as his black eyes watched their progress. As much as William wanted to yell at the man he knew it would only get him punished. Bernard had fought at the Duke's side during the recent crusade into the Holy Land and knew more of fighting then most men of forty-five years.

"Fight smarter---not harder," Bernard called again. He crossed his arms and leaned back into the shadow of the wall and waited for them to continue.

William and Conrad crossed the small dirt area four more times before Bernard called a halt to the mock battle and had them place their practice swords in the small rack. Already it was mid-morning and there were still many chores that needed to be done.

"Your father wants you to help clear the south field again," Bernard called as they downed great gulps of water from a waiting container of cool liquid.

"Again?" William complained. "We just did it last week."

"The rain two days ago uncovered more," Bernard answered evenly.

William gulped and nodded; when that look of steel entered Bernard's eyes he knew better then to argue. Together he and Conrad exited the grounds inside the wall of the small keep and entered the village clustered along the road.

"Why do you always push?" Conrad asked as they trudged along nodding to those who greeted them.

"You're not my father," William muttered back as he studied the ground under his feet. "Don't act like you are. I am thirteen already, don't treat me like a baby."

The village was home to about four hundred people, not including children, and all of them worked for the master of the manor. William never thought of his father as a powerful person but he was greatly respected and well liked by all that lived on their family grounds.

"They are starting already," Conrad said as he pointed to the cluster of eight men and women that gathered near a small stand of trees on the edge of the freshly plowed field.

William ignored his brother and scampered to one of the tallest trees and started climbing. He would start when he felt like it, not when his brother told him to.

"Come on William, we need to start," Conrad said loudly. He frowned at his brother but finally decided to ignore him and turned to the field where the rest of the laborers were starting to pick the exposed rocks and haul them to the partial fence. The stones would be used to build the barrier along the road to keep smaller animals from destroying the crops which would soon be planted.

William scrambled to the top of the tree and looked south to where Clair's family manor dominated the hill almost two leagues in that direction. There were signs of movement in several of the fields that lay on their lands but he didn't see the familiar figure of his best friend anywhere.

He looked down and noticed that his brother was glaring up at him so he climbed back down and set his boots off to the side. Picking stones was dirty work and he did not want to ruin one of his last good pair of leather boots.

The stones were not very numerous but they seemed to have come up at the furthest points from the fence they were repairing. William grabbed the first one and grunted under the weight. The ground was soft and clung to his feet as he walked towards the distant fence. This was going to be a long day; he could feel it already.

The field work took most of the day and when the rocks were finally cleared the sun was beginning to set. William and Conrad carried their boots as they walked back to the manor.

"I hate picking rocks," William muttered.

"You like to eat, don't you?" Conrad replied in a superior tone.

William ignored him and walked to where the men they had worked with that day were pulling pails of water out of the deep well in the middle of the village. It took several buckets of water each to rinse the dirt away and by time each of them was clean the sun was almost under the horizon. High above them the last rays of light on the clouds created a brilliant arrangement of colors.

"I am famished," William muttered.

They trudged through the gate in the thick wall that surrounded the small manor building and nodded to the archer, who kept watch from the tower above the gate. The wall was only ten feet tall and the tower sat above it by another ten feet offering the archer an open view of the approaches to the manor. The front door of the manor was propped open and the smell of roast beef and fried potatoes filtered out into the evening air. William's mouth began to water immediately and his stomach growled loudly.

Inside the building was a long table that dominated the front room and it was surrounded by chairs. As they entered, William could see that the table was heavily laden with food. Already a dozen people were gathered and so they hurried to their seats near Bernard.

While they waited for the last of the seats to be filled, William looked across the table to where his mother sat. She had her dark hair pulled back and the laugh lines showed around her green eyes. The Duke was sitting next to her with the great leather bound copy of the Holy Scriptures in his hands. It was the original copy of the smaller copy that his father had passed to him. It was written in Lantium, the original language of the Holy land and his lips moved as he read the words to himself.

"We are ready, my love."

The Duke looked up at his wife and smiled at her. Reverently he closed the Holy Book and then turned to the table and motioned wide with his hands. "Let us give thanks for this bountiful meal."

William folded his hands and closed his eyes hoping that his father would not be long winded. His stomach was growling almost constantly now and the plate before him smelled heavenly. Thankfully the prayer was short and the moment his father ended it he grabbed his wooden spoon and attacked his plate like a wolf loosed among the lambs.

"How did the work in the south field

go?" the Duke asked Conrad. The Duke ate slowly and with measured bites.

"Well enough," Conrad replied. "I think it is ready for planting." Conrad paused in his headlong run through his first plate of food and spoke around the bite in his mouth.

"Good," the Duke said with a smile. He reached out to where Conrad and sat and patted him on the shoulder.

"And what of you, William," the Duke said with a smile dancing around his lips. "Did you see anything from your perch atop the tree today?"

"No, Father," William said sheepishly. He glared at Conrad sure that his brother had betrayed his trip to the top of the oak, but the older sibling simply shrugged his shoulders and returned to his plate.

"Ah, glare not at your brother so," the Duke chuckled. "It was Bernard that spotted movement atop the tree and told me. Just promise me you will be careful going that high."

"Oh, I will Father, you know I will," William said earnestly.

"Now then I want you all to be careful over the next few days," the Duke instructed. The casual conversation at the table slowed and finally faded to complete silence and all waited for him to explain.

"The thief, Scar Face, escaped from the King's dungeon a few days ago." the Duke said. "I don't know if he even knows who I am but it is better to be safe then sorry. William," the Duke narrowed his eyes at him. "No long trips by yourself. I want you escorted by one of Bernard's men."

"Yes, Father," William knew by the tone of his father voice that there was no negotiating on this point. He would have to follow his father's words to the letter if he wanted to avoid getting in serious trouble.

2 – The Plan

The next few days came and went quietly and William took pains to avoid going anywhere by himself. Still, one of Bernard's men trailed after him and despite the attempt to remain out of the way, William had that watched over and hunted feeling.

At first he thought it was rather fun and all a bit mysterious but after a while it became annoying. He took to ducking around corners quickly and hiding himself in the smallest places he could until the worried face of his follower rounded the corner looking for him.

"Young sir," the man finally erupted. "You must stop doing that. I am tasked by your father to follow you and that is what I must do."

William just smiled and ducked his head as he sprinted for the end of the alley. Just before he found freedom a strong hand caught him and he was yanked to a halt.

"Now then, shall we go see your father?" the soldier asked grimly.

"Alright, I will stop," William grunted as the strong hand lifted him clear off the ground and pulled him around so that he could see the gruff face of his guardian.

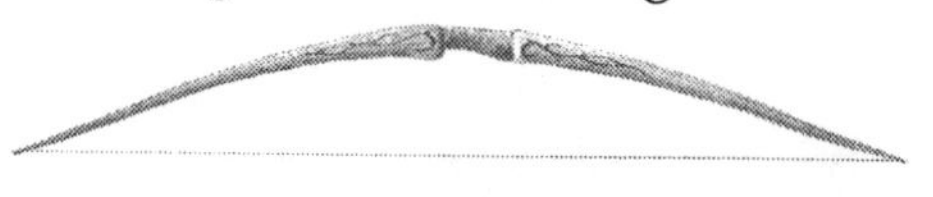

On Sunday his family gathered in a small stone chapel situated between his father's lands and Clair's family lands.

They left the manor when the sun was still rising over the nearby trees and walked quietly to the south. The chapel was built of sturdy stone walls and its roof was held aloft by large beams cut in the Parval woods and hauled to the site by teams of oxen.

The priest was a devoted man who defied church law on a regular basis and challenged his flock to read the scriptures and search for the Savior's truths in the hallowed pages of the Holy Book. He spoke for nearly two hours that morning and when he finally completed the service William was close to falling asleep for the third time. Just as his eyes were drifting shut the priest motioned for them to stand and William scrambled to his feet.

"Amen."

"Amen," the small congregation replied. With the service finished it was time to renew friendships and pass news of what had happened in the neighboring lands, this gave William and Clair time to talk finally.

Now that the grown ups were busy with their conversation, talk between William and Clair soon turned to mischief. Each had grand ideas of what adventures awaited them if they could just get away from the parents.

"How can we go explore the old cave if you have Bernard's men watching you every minute of the day?" Clair asked. She pulled a strand of her blond hair forward and chewed on it as her blue eyes darted around and watched for anyone trying to over hear their conversation.

"Nothing has happened and I think Father will relax soon," William insisted. "We can go there on Tuesday when everyone else is out planting. That is the day I am supposed to be with Fredrick practicing my archery."

"Won't he notice?" Clair asked curiously. She had only heard stories of the old Freglander who lived on their lands and tended a small garden of herbs. Besides being a miracle worker with the herbs, he was an accomplished archer and was tasked with training the Duke's men and supplying them with bows and arrows.

"No, he lets me run around all of the time when I am there," William said in hushed tones. That was a bit of information that he definitely did not want anyone else to know. He looked around as he noticed Conrad looking at them but he stuck his tongue out at his brother until he turned away in disgust. "I can go for a while and then tell him I am going home. We can have most of the day to explore."

William knew that it would take them an hour to walk to where the old cave entrance and its mysterious depths waited for them near the old mill pond. The manor house was abandoned and the lands it once stood on now belonged to the crown. Talk had been circulated lately of a new master coming to work the lands but nothing had happened yet and William wanted to be the first, in his mind, to explore the depths of the cave.

"I can bring several torches," Clair volunteered. She tapped a finger against the inside of her other hand as she counted off what they would need.

"I will bring some food from Fredrick's and a coil of rope," William replied. He fell silent as Conrad walked up to them and looked down at them with a cocked head.

"What are you two planning?" he asked suspiciously.

"Nothing, go away," William blustered as he scowled at Conrad. His scowl deepened when Clair blushed and smiled at Conrad. He wished his brother would just go away before he ruined everything.

"Clair, don't let him talk you into anything crazy," Conrad said with a sigh. "I really hope all this whispering has nothing to do with the mill pond cave."

"Go away," William responded sullenly.

"It does, doesn't it," Conrad said with a shake of his head. "You know Father told you to stay away from that place, it's dangerous."

"Don't you ever want to do anything exciting," William burst out. He jumped at how loud his own voice sounded and then turned away quickly as his father looked up from his conversation with Clair's father and looked questioningly at them.

"Sure I do," Conrad replied. "That is why I am coming with you two, someone with a brain in his head has to keep you both from killing yourselves. Since no one else is volunteering it might as well be me."

William stopped and frowned, that had not gone how he wanted it to go. He hoped that if he was alone with Clair he could cement their relationship with a kiss, if he was lucky. Now he had to contend with his nosy brother ruining all of his carefully laid plans.

"When are we going?" Conrad asked.

"None of your business," William said in a panicked tone. "Just go away."

"Tuesday," Clair said with a winning smile. "This will be so much fun. Maybe I can convince Charles to come with us too." She clapped her hands together excitedly.

"Oh great, lets invite everyone while we are at it," William said as his heart sank into his boots. That would end it all, there was no chance of doing anything else but exploring.

As much as he wanted to stay angry, William soon found that he was happy that Conrad was coming along. Once his older brother joined the expedition and stood with them in the chapel yard, his father must have decided that nothing malicious was being planned and he returned to his conversation.

The planning went well from there on and soon their small expedition was arranged and all of the supplies spoken for. They parted that afternoon with plans of gathering at the mill pond at two hours after sunrise on Tuesday.

Monday went by slowly with William moving quickly through his chores and creeping about the manor searching for things that they would need. First he found a fifty foot length of rope and secreted it in the stump of the old oak tree on the far side of the north field.

He was leaving his father's small armory with a dagger when he was caught by the ear and spun around.

"And what are you doing with that?" Bernard demanded. His eyes flashed to the steel dagger in William's hand.

"Nothing..." William knew that his answer was wrong the moment he gave it.

"Try again," Bernard said as his eyes narrowed. His grip on William's ear tightened even more.

"Look, I just want to try and carve a little horse for Clair," William lied quickly. Oddly he saw Bernard's face soften.

"Is that what all this sneaking around is about?" Bernard asked. He laughed and shook his head, "You both like her, don't you? Well, go on boy, but make sure that dagger is back here quickly. And you can sharpen it when you are done."

William stared in amazement as Bernard laughed one more time and then turned and walked away leaving him with the dagger. He had never seen the soldier bend his father's rules about the handling of weapons once, until now. Suddenly William realized he was still standing in full view holding a weapon that he was not supposed to have, so he tucked the dagger under his shirt and scurried away.

By that evening all was in place and William was as excited as he had ever been. Conrad was strangely silent at supper and hardly looked at him, even worse they didn't argue once and both father and mother looked at them suspiciously. Thankfully, no one asked them any questions and they were freed to go to their beds soon after supper.

William lay in bed that night for nearly an hour before sleep finally came. There was a small voice in his mind that kept telling him that what he was doing was wrong, but he steadfastly ignored the feeling and finally managed to quiet it.

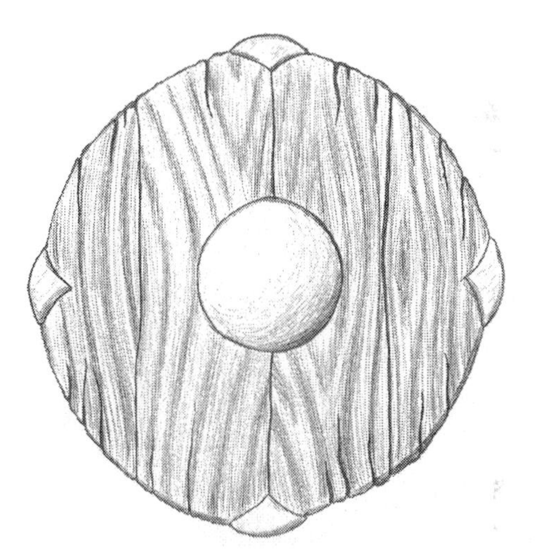

3 – Old Mill Pond

Tuesday dawned with a brilliant burst of sunshine and William leapt out of bed, donned his cleanest set of clothes, and ran downstairs. His bedroom was on the upper floor and when he arrived in the kitchen, his father looked up from the leather bound Holy Book and smiled at him.

"Are you going to Fredrick's today?" the Duke asked quietly. His voice seemed to contain a hint of a question.

"Yes, Father," William said as he kicked at the floor. For a moment his conscious tormented him but he pushed the feeling away and grabbed a thick slice of bread from the wooden table. Hurried, he shoved it into his mouth so that he would not have to say anything else.

"Good, I have business today outside the manor and I will not be home until late," the Duke said. "Have a good day and remember to say your prayers and read the scriptures tonight."

William nodded as he continued to cringe on the inside, why did his father have to pick this moment to remind him of his scripture readings.

He gave his father a great hug and then grabbed his small bow and quiver of practice arrows from the table, where he had set them down, and bolted for the door. When he arrived at the gate Conrad was already waiting and the two of them took off running for the far side of the northern most field of their lands.

When they arrived at the old stump they found all of their supplies in place and quickly divided them up. From there it was two leagues through thick forest to Fredrick's house perched on the edge of a wide meadow. Stone fences marked off the edges of his herb gardens and a babbling brook brought a steady supply of fresh water to the gardens.

"Both of you today?"

William smiled at the quavering voice as it reached them from the front of the cottage. Fredrick stepped from the wooden door and smiled at them. He was white-haired and his great mustache and beard was filled with nearly as much white as his hair.

"We have not got time to practice today, Fredrick," Conrad said importantly. "We are in the middle of an important errand." Conrad puffed out his chest as he talked and William rolled his eyes.

"Oh, you are," Fredrick said as his voice fell. Disappointment filled his face as he looked at them. "Well, I suppose I can tend my garden today instead of teaching you more about archery. I will have your new bows ready soon."

"Can we see them?" William said excitedly. He hoped that the new bow would be ready soon; the one he was using now was too small for his arms.

"Sure, come in if you have a moment."

The two boys followed Fredrick into the small work shop built into the back of his cottage and looked around at the collection of bows and arrows. There were at least twenty bows in various states of completion but on the workbench were two nearly complete bows.

They talked for a few minutes with the old archer and then took their leave and trotted down the forest trail to the west. The trail led them along the edge of the meadow and William could not help but enjoy the myriads of wild flowers growing around them.

Waiting for them on the edge of the forest was Clair and her older brother Charles. He was a year older then William and Clair and nearly as tall as Conrad. Between them they carried a pair of leather packs and two torches each, the thick lengths of oak were wrapped in cloth and soaked in a flammable liquid.

They continued down the trail laughing and talking as they walked, each of them imagining the fun they were about to have. William hung back and let Conrad and Charles lead down the path while he walked next to Clair and chatted with her.

"Does your dad suspect anything?" Clair asked.

"I don't think so," William bragged. "I was pretty careful about my preparations."

"Me too," Clair said with a blush. "I felt kind of bad about lying to them but I don't know... I guess it went away after a while."

The walk to the mill pond took them an hour but they finally arrived at the overgrown remains of what had once been a village. In some nameless battle many years ago, the village had been burned to the ground and all that remained was the stone walls of the mill. The ruins were situated in a small bowl-like depression and above it, staring down at them, were the moss covered wall of the old fortress. The Black Brier Manor had been sacked years ago when tribes of nomads from the Wilds to the north had pushed south looking for treasure and plunder. They were only stopped when the Duke and the Baron of Corduval joined forces to stop them. William stared up the empty manor house mesmerized with the thought of someday exploring its depths, but at the same time an ominous feeling swept over him. The house looked sad to him as if it was mourning for someone to return and live in it. Finally William turned his attention back to the mill pond.

The pond was overgrown with weeds and slime and the songs of bullfrogs and insects filled the air. Around them bulrushes and cattails grew in abundance and blocked out entire sections of the water.

"Cool," William muttered as he leaned over the water and tried to grab a frog. The amphibian leapt off the lily pad where he was sitting and vanished in the water with a tremendous leap. William stumbled back as the two older boys collapsed in gales of laughter at his near soaking.

"Come on, let's find the cave," Conrad said when he could finally stand again.

William glared at them but then a smile finally broke over his face and he joined in the laughter. They walked to the remains of the mill and found a small game trail that circled the ponds. It took them two trips around the pond before they spotted the dark entrance to the cave. The mill pond was built into the side of a rocky hill and the cave entrance was hidden from sight behind a stand of willows.

"Back here," William called. He beamed with pride that he was the one that had found it. He shoved through the willows and stood in the entrance to the darkness. The mouth was about four paces across and it was low enough that they were forced to bend over to enter. The air in the entrance to the cave was cool as they stepped out of the sun and it all seemed so mysterious.

"Let me light a torch," Conrad muttered as he took an old knife and a piece of flint from his pack. He hit the flint four times before the sparks fell on the specially prepared head of the torch. Charles blew on the spark and, after a second, the tightly wrapped torch caught fire and blazed to life.

"Here, light one more," Charles said as he handed a second torch to Clair.

When they had two blazing torches they bent over and slipped inside the darkness. The entrance to the cave went down quickly and they were forced to climb down a long narrow passage until it finally opened up.

"This is amazing," William muttered. His hand went nervously to the dagger at his waist and his fingers wrapped around the hilt. Suddenly, he let go as Clair reached over and grabbed his wrist. Her hand slipped into his and she looked at him with wide eyes.

"This is so wonderful," Clair said excitedly. The cavern stretched out under the hillside and then seemed to break into two separate tunnels and they vanished even further into the ground. The one they chose to explore stopped after a dozen paces and they were forced to backtrack to the main cave and try the second one.

"It looks like there is a path here," Conrad whispered. He pointed down at the floor where a bit of old cloth had fallen to the ground in some bygone time. He reached out to pick up the cloth but it fell to pieces as his fingers touched it.

Since the torches were still going strong, they crawled across several narrow parts of the passage until it opened up again. This time the room that they found was a large circular area and they all stopped and stared in surprise. In the middle of the room was a hide covered dwelling with a bit of sunshine filtering in through a hole in the roof above.

"Someone lives here!" Clair said in a strangled voice. She looked around and immediately grabbed onto William's hand again.

"It looks old," Conrad said as they walked over to the frame of sticks and old hides that covered the sticks. There was an old fire pit in front of the entrance to the tent and the bits of blackened wood fell apart easily. "I don't think anyone stays here anymore."

"No heat in the coals," Charles said as he stood back to his feet.

"Do you want to go into the tent?" William asked?

"No!" Clair erupted as she pulled him back a step. "What happens if something is inside?"

"Oh, nothing is inside," Charles said with a laugh. Despite his brave words none of them wanted to be the first to look inside and so they stood nervously around the cave. There was another passage that went down into the earth at a steep angle but there was a cool breeze coming up from the passage and it made their torches flicker wildly each time they tried to work deeper into the earth.

"Well, shall we start back?" Clair asked finally. The trip had been fun but she was tired of being under ground, and wanted to explore around the ruined village.

"No, I am going to look inside the tent," William said suddenly. He had this one chance to prove his bravery and he was going to take it. He strode to the front of the tent and faced the leather flap with a determined look. The skins that covered the front half of the tent looked to be some sort of great cat that was covered with spots. The one hanging in front of the entrance was that of a lion with his head and paws held up.

"Don't, William," Clair begged. She reached out and grabbed his hand again and tried to drag him back.

"Chicken," Conrad muttered with a smirk on his face. He laughed at the irritated look that erupted onto William's face.

That was all it took for William. His faced hardened and he pulled his hand free of Clair and smiled at her.

"I will be right back," William said forcefully and then he pushed back the tent flap and stepped inside.

4 – Black Brier Estate

William stepped into the tent and felt like he had entered another world. He slipped to the ground and his eyes shut as sleep closed in on him, oddly his mind stayed awake with a dream unlike any he had ever had before. The inside of the tent faded almost immediately and he felt like he was falling head over heels. Suddenly, he landed with a thud on a dark hillside and his eyes went wide as he looked around. There were a few stunted trees scattered along the hill; but for the most part, it was covered with course grass and a warm breeze blew up from the valley below.

"Hello!" William cried out in a panic. He whirled around and was amazed to see the small leather hut at the top of the hill behind him. It mirrored the one he had stepped into just moments before in everyway. Suddenly a voice spoke.

"Why are you here?"

William whirled about, stumbled back, and fell to his haunches as a voice spoke behind him. There was an old woman standing on the hillside behind him looking at him curiously. She was dressed in a long robe that covered her from head to toe and her face was weathered from years of exposure to the sun and wind.

"If *they* find you here *they* will hurt you," she said. She shook her head as if not believing how foolish the boy was being.

"Who?" William blurted out. "Where am I?" Panic was filling his mind as he clutched at the dagger in his belt. He needed to find a way to protect himself and return home, and he wanted to do it all quickly.

"You are in their hidden valley and they don't like visitors." She reached out, took his hand, and helped him to his feet. "Follow me quickly."

Her face was friendly so William took her hand, stood, and followed her back to the small tent. Before they entered he looked around and suddenly realized that there was a deep valley below them; and at the bottom of the valley was a thick walled fortress that sprawled out and covered a great swath of ground. Dark pendants flew from the towers and a sense of despair seemed to fill the air around the fortress.

"What is that?" William asked as he pulled her to a halt and stepped back towards the castle. His curiosity was aroused and despite the strangeness of the place and his journey here, he was anxious to explore.

"Now is not the time," the old woman repeated as she shoved him towards the tent once again. "Listen to me, son, I think you will return here someday. For now you must grow and become a man. Now go, and beware the scarred man, he means to do your family great harm."

William stumbled backwards back into the hide covered tent and suddenly darkness closed in around him again.

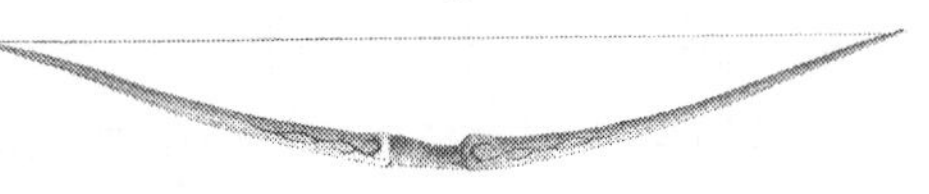

"William!"

He woke slowly to the sound of his voice being called over and over. Someone was searching for him. Weakly, he climbed to his feet and looked around; he was inside the rough tent. On the ground was a small mat for sleeping and a jar for holding water. The jar was cracked nearly in half and he crawled blindly towards the door. All he wanted was to see his family. His mind was foggy about what had taken place over the last few minutes and he struggled to recall all of what had happened.

"William!"

Another shout echoed around the entrance to the tent and suddenly he was free of the tent and looking around in the darkness. Above him the hole. where the cavern touched the surface, was dark. Voices were calling for him and the voices came from above he realized.

"I am here!" William called out hoping that someone was nearby. He directed his voice towards the opening overhead and called out again.

"William?" the Duke shouted.

"Father?" William said in disbelief. The secret journey to the cave came flooding back to him all at once and suddenly a healthy dose of fear filled his mind. *Why is my father here?* He thought.

"Where are you son?"

William suddenly realized that his father's voice was echoing down weakly from the surface and he scrambled over until he was directly underneath the opening.

"I am down here, Father," William cried out again. He heard a scrambling of feet and voices and suddenly Bernard's face appeared for just a moment above the opening.

"Bernard, I see you!" William shouted and he was rewarded a moment later with the return of the soldier's solemn face.

"I found him, sire," Bernard called as he stood up and waved to where the Duke was standing. Next to him stood Conrad, Clair, Charles, and five men from their estate.

Including the six men Bernard had brought the woods were suddenly alive as people rushed to where he was standing.

"There is a hole in the ground," Bernard motioned to the ground. "We should widen it just a bit and then lower him a rope." The rest nodded and began to carefully remove some of the stones and dirt surrounding the narrow hole. Suddenly, William realized that there were several stone arches built into the cave to help support the ground above and the place became even more mysterious in his mind.

William waited breathlessly in the dark cavern hearing suddenly every bit of every sound echoed back at him. He jumped when a pair of bats suddenly entered the cave and swooped around for a moment before continuing on into the night sky.

"Here comes the rope," Bernard called. He dropped the thick strand of rope through the hole and looked down into the darkness. "Tie it around your waist and we will pull you out."

William reached up excitedly when the rope finally reached where he stood. He looped it around his body under his arms and cinched it down tight. After looping it several times around itself, he tied off a strong knot and called back, "I am ready. Pull me up." His voice shook as he tried to calm his nerves and failed.

A few showers of dirt and bumped elbows later, he was standing on the earth once more as his father looked down at him.

"Where were you!" Conrad said, his voice was nearly a shout. He grabbed William and seemed torn between giving him a hug and wringing his neck. "We shouted for you in that cave for an hour before we ran home to get dad and Bernard."

"What do you mean? I was only in the tent for a couple of minutes," William insisted as he tried to shrug away from his brother. He looked to Clair for help but she kept her eyes low and seemed more interested in the grass then in helping him.

"Son, it is very late," the Duke replied in a quiet voice. "If I can believe the story Conrad has told me, you have been missing for nearly half the day."

"But… No…," William stammered as he struggled to remember what had happened. "I… I can't remember exactly what happened but it can't be half the day gone." Still, as much as he protested, when he looked up the sun was gone from the sky and the moon was rising quickly. Surrounding the full moon was a myriad of stars that one normally only saw when in the country and away from the constant lights burning in the village.

"Come on we have found our wayward sheep," the Duke said in a calm voice. "Let us go home and deal with their punishment for disobedience tomorrow."

"But…" William stammered once more and then he stopped. It was pointless to argue that he had learned his lesson.

"Sons, you both disobeyed my rule and put Clair and the others in great danger," the Duke replied. "We will deal with all of this tomorrow, including your older brother who should have known much better."

Suddenly, there was the clopping of hooves and a series of shouts as Bernard's men and Clair's protectors fell back into a defensive circle facing out. From the ruins of the mill across the meadow, a line of horsemen erupted led by a man wearing heavy armor and carrying a long lance made of wood but tipped with iron.

They crossed the distance between them in a flash and soon a score of lances were all aimed at their throats.

"Why are you trespassing on Black Brier Estate?" the man in the armor asked. "You have no right to be here."

"I am sorry, sire, but my son fell down an old hole in this field and we have just now found and rescued him," the Duke replied evenly. Despite the disadvantage in numbers he spoke calmly and with assurance. "We were under the impression that the old mill area was unclaimed and belonged to the crown."

"It has been given to me by the king and you will leave now," the knight replied and his tone left little room for argument.

"As you wish," the Duke replied.

"Trespass on my lands again and I will speak to the king about this matter."

The duke's face reddened slightly at the implied insult but he nodded and motioned Bernard and his men to put up their weapons. "There is no need for bloodshed, he is within his right as land holder to make us leave."

William turned with his father and walked quickly from the area of the old mill pond and did not stop until they were passing Fredrick's cabin. It took them until the moon was high in the sky to return home and he and Conrad were immediately sent to their beds without supper.

"We will deal with this in the morning," the Duke said as he ordered them to bed. He disappeared a moment later into his own chambers and closed the door behind him as he vanished.

"We messed up big time," Conrad muttered as he started to trudge up the steps to his room.

"I don't see what the big deal is,"

William replied as he followed Conrad up the steps.

"We disobeyed William, dad trusted us and we disobeyed him," Conrad said with a sad look in his eyes. "We really messed up."

William shook his head and walked by Conrad to where the door to his room waited for him. Oh, he knew they had not listened but it seemed to be such a petty thing. Why did his father have to be such a spoilsport?

5 – Parval Forest

The rest of the summer passed slowly for William. He did not see Clair except on Sundays and that was only for short periods of time. His father seemed bent on extracting every bit of manual labor that was possible from him and Conrad. They spent from morning to night laboring in the fields with the rest of the hired hands and even their weapons training was put on hold.

"Are we ever going to be able to train with our swords again?" William ventured one day while they were trudging to a field north of the manor. It seemed to him that every field on their land had suddenly gained the ability to grow full of weeds over night. Sadly the only job that they seemed able to do was pull weeds; his hands were covered with green stains that no amount of washing would remove.

"Sometime, yes," Conrad replied.

William glared over at Conrad and shook his head at the sad sound to his voice. Conrad had turned seventeen four days ago and the celebration had been a dull, almost boring, party. At least their father was beginning to lessen their loads. Instead of working from sunup to sunset, they were allowed to rest for an hour during the hottest part of the day.

Although, William figured that it had more to do with the hot conditions then with a change on his father's part. When it cooled they would be going from sunup to sun down again.

They spent the morning pulling weeds from the rapidly growing field of vegetables that included tomatoes, carrots, and beans. It was early afternoon when the men working furthest to the east, where the road leading south from the Dukes lands was visible, raised a shout of alarm. Two of them stood on the stone fence waving their hands wildly.

"What is it?" William asked as he stood up wearily and tried to stretch the kinks from his back.

"I don't know," Conrad replied. "Let's go find out."

William breathed a sigh of relief. Even his stalwart brother, who seemed bent on punishing himself, was beginning to break under the boredom. They jogged to the far side of the field and climbed up on the stone wall. Down the road they could see a line of tired and worn people carrying what little possessions they still had on their backs.

"Where are you from?" Conrad asked as he jumped down and approached the soot covered man who led the group.

"The hamlet of Clantonbury," the man said as he shook his head. "A group of bandits burned our village last night and took everything of value. They left most of us alive and told us to walk this way or they would kill us."

William was shocked but he frowned when Conrad motioned for the survivors to follow him. "Where are you going?" William asked.

"I am going to take them to Father and see if we can help them," Conrad replied. "They are from a village on our lands; it is our duty."

"Why?" William muttered. True, their manor was prosperous, but he did not think that they could provide for a massive influx of new mouths to feed. It was the outlying villages that added much of the food and trade goods that they relied on.

"Because it is the right thing to do, William," Conrad said simply. He turned and motioned for the group of thirty of so people to follow him back down the lane to where the manor graced its hilltop.

William jumped back down off the fence and motioned to the others around him to follow him back out into the field. They had work to get done and he wanted to be done with it so he could find a place to lie down and rest before father gave him more chores to do.

It was late afternoon when William finally made his way home. He had found a spot of shade under a willow tree and managed to get a quick nap. Now feeling refreshed but hungry, he jogged down the lane and wondered what Conrad was doing. His brother had not returned to help with the rest of the field and that irked him.

When he arrived in the village there was a rush of activity around him and he saw a score of new shelters and rough cottages taking shape. It seemed that the entire village was caught up in the effort to help the new arrivals. People rushed everywhere carrying goods and food while others carried timber and nails from the storage sheds to where the buildings were taking shape.

"Ah, William, there you are," the Duke said when he saw his youngest son finally wander into the village. "Here, take this jug of water and bundle of food to the north field. I have four men posted near the edge of our property to keep watch for any trouble."

"But, Father, I am hungry too," William complained as the bundles were passed to him.

"Son, we have plenty to eat and will do so soon," the Duke replied. "These folk have nothing and are in need of our help, looking to the needs of others is what marks our faith. Someday you will stand before your Maker and answer for your actions, always remember that."

William frowned as his father gave him a pat on the head and a gentle shove back down the road that he had just traveled. Finally he turned around and ignored the growl in his stomach and started towards the northern field.

The next morning William was left to himself much of the day and decided to see what Clair was doing. With his brother and father so pre-occupied, it was the perfect time to visit his friend.

He walked the hard packed dirt lane south and east from their manor and skipped small rocks off the top of the fence. There were many people out in the fields and he waved happily to each.

"Thank goodness I am not out there," William muttered happily to himself. It was a beautiful day, the sun was shining and a light breeze was drifting along bringing a bit of much needed coolness to the lands. It took him less then an hour to reach Clair's family manor; when he arrived he knocked on the door, and waited impatiently.

"Is Clair here?" William asked the woman who answered the door of the Baron's house. Clair's father was a noble of an old bloodline and most people simply called him the Baron.

"No, little sir, she is down by the stream with her brother fishing."

William nodded his thanks and turned around from the massive oaken door. Clair's house was slightly bigger then his, but the village clustered around the protective walls was a bit smaller. Everything here was built of timber except for the small castle and the walls surrounding it. The estate was almost twice the size of Duke Edwards and there were eight villages scattered across his lands.

He trotted across the courtyard and waved to the man watching the only approach to the castle and headed out the gate. The stream in question was half a league further south and the thought of fishing sounded like a great idea.

"If Charles is there I bet he has an extra pole too," William said aloud as he jogged south down a narrow trail between two fences. It took him another few minutes to reach the stream and spot the familiar figures of his friends sitting on the bank of the water. Clair was leaned back and her fishing pole was lying off to the side while her line floated lazily in the water. It was obvious to his trained eye that her hook had been cleaned off but she didn't seem to care.

Across the water about twenty steps to the south, the border of the Parval forest filled the countryside. William could still hear his father's stern warning about the dangers of the Parval Forest echoing in his mind. Still, his father was so far away and it seemed like such an interesting place to explore.

"Doesn't look that bad," William muttered as he slipped down the banks of the creek and waved to Clair.

"Hi, how are you doing?" William said happily as he plopped down beside her. The trees offered a good bit of shade here and the weather was perfect.

"Shh, you will scare the fish away," Charles muttered crossly as he pointed to where a pair of silvery forms lay on the bank next to him. "I got two already."

"Can I try?" William asked. When Charles nodded he looked around until he spotted a willow branch nearby that was perfect for his purpose.

Using Charles's knife he cut the pole and freed it of twigs, then with a bit of borrowed string and a rough hook he was ready. The stream widened and slowed as it opened into a deep pool under the fishing hole and the water was so clear they caught glimpses of the silvery shadows as they slipped by under the surface.

They fished for nearly an hour and caught several small fish before William bored of the sport.

"Let's go look inside the forest," William suggested. He tossed his pole down and looked over to Clair and Charles.

"Father says it is dangerous in the dark parts of the woods," Clair replied. Still there was a gleam in her eye that said she wanted to explore.

"So we stay out of the dark parts."

Charles snorted loudly and looked over at them, "Remember what happened last time you two went exploring."

Clair put down her pole and stuck out her tongue at the back of his head drawing a snicker from William.

"Come on, that was an accident."

"Ya it was an accident," Clair said mimicking William.

"Don't say I didn't warn you," Charles said as he yanked his pole up and hooked into a fish. A broad smile covered his face as he grabbed onto the string and began pulling it in hand over hand.

William and Clair ignored the rest of

what he was saying as they made their way down stream to where a series of stones would get them across the water. Once they were on the proper side of that barrier, they advanced on the woods, talking about the things they would see and the unexplored places they would visit.

"I bet there are all sorts of wild animals just waiting for us to see them," William said excitedly. He and Clair stopped at the edge of the forest and looked up at the massive branches of the oak trees. The trees stared back without saying a word except for the occasional scraping of branches together that seemed to say 'stay out'.

William shook away the imagined warning of the tree branches and took a step forward. What could possibly be bad about looking around at the edge of the trees. It wasn't like they were going to spend days in the forest.

"Come on, let's go," Clair said as she stepped by him. She grabbed his hand and pulled towards the forest.

As they entered the trees, the limbs above them came together to block out the sun and all around them quiet settled. A few birds chirped here and there but except for the sounds of their own voices nothing else moved.

"What now?" Clair asked when they had walked a score of steps into the woods. Behind them they could still see the edge of the forest and the stream in the distance. The distant figure of Charles looked up once but he remained where he was, staring at the sparkling waters and his fishing line.

I don't know," William looked around. He wanted to be able to explore but he was getting nervous about venturing too far from the safety of the stream. "What about that hill over there?" He pointed to the east into the thicker part of the woods where the trees blocked out the sun completely and silence reigned. There was a rise just visible through the trees and he thought it would be a fun spot to look at.

"It looks like there is an old building there," Clair said. "Father never told me that anyone lived here." She could just barely make out the squared off section of a stone wall through the tree trunks.

Carefully and quietly they made their way across the forest floor, walking around ferns and a few scattered tangles of underbrush until they reached the hill.

Rocks and boulders jutted out on all sides and offered an easy method of climbing so they started up. When they neared the top William could see that the remains of a small castle were tumbled about the top of the hill. All was quiet as he and Clair crept slowly over the jumble of stones that had once been a gatehouse and found themselves in an open area where the sun still worked its way to the ground. Before the structure of the ancient keep, the gate house kept watch over the vines and saplings that erupted from the windows and doors.

"What is that?" William said suddenly as he pointed to where a bit of color caught his eye. They hurried over to an overhang that was formed of the fallen stones and slipped into the deepest part of the shadows that they could. The air was cool under the overhang and the two stood close to each other as they watched the courtyard.

Suddenly the sound of voices reached them and they listened even though the view of the speakers was blocked by the stones.

"The Duke that lives nearby," the first voice said in a raspy tone. "He is the one we seek."

"This I know," replied the second

person.

William noticed that the second voice sounded cultured and refined, almost like his father but more sinister.

"He is a busy body and will interrupt our plans if he learns of them. What shall we do?" the first voice asked.

"Keep gathering your men and stick to the plans we have laid down," the second replied. "This place is perfect for our operations. It is distant enough from the king to be safe and yet close enough to give us access to what we need."

There was a shuffle of footsteps and suddenly the second voice spoke again.

"Do try and control your men and your own need to pillage and plunder," the voice turned ominous. "It will draw unwanted attention to our more profitable activities."

"That Duke ruined my plans once," the first voice complained. "I want revenge."

"And you shall have it but not until I am ready."

The two sets of footsteps faded and William looked over at Clair who was staring back at him with wide eyes. They were both shaking at the strange conversation they had just heard.

When the silence was unbroken for a long time, they finally ventured out and ran for the edge of the forest.

"What do we do?" Clair asked breathlessly as they emerged from the trees.

"Are you kidding me, don't tell anyone," William burst out. "We would get in so much trouble. Promise me you will never speak of this to anyone."

"I promise," Clair replied. Deep inside she did not think this was a good course to take but she trusted William.

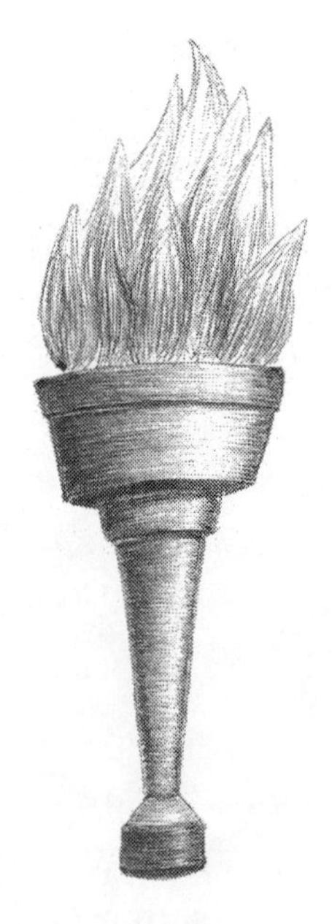

6 – Baldtop Peak

Another six months passed before the next incident happened and William was finally getting used to the group of new-comers. Most of the villagers, it seemed, had lived nearby for years and yet he did not know any of them. There were two boys his age that moved into the village and he met them almost immediately. They spent what time they could together. His father's eye on him was lessening but he still received enough chores to keep him busy most days.

There were three villages on their ancestral lands and the smallest of these was Quiet Meadows about a mile west of the manor. The land rose sharply in that direction and was well suited for sheep and so Quiet

Meadows and the fifty or so souls who lived there tended the Duke's rather extensive herds of sheep.

Conrad and William were in the practice yard once again at work with their wooden swords when there was a rush of footsteps outside the gate. They had only recently returned to their training and were working hard to regain lost skills.

"Watch your stance, William," Bernard called from the shade of the wall. He was sitting on a wooden bench and his blue eyes were locked on them as they battled across the dusty training area. "You need to keep your feet separated more or you will lose your balance." The constant barrage of advice from the warrior annoyed him but still he knew that Bernard was right. If he lost his balance he would be at the mercy of his opponent.

William grunted as he glanced down and realized a second later the mistake of doing so. A moment later Conrad's wooden sword slapped his side and his breath left him in a sudden explosion of air. A few small stars appeared before his eyes and he held up his hands in a gesture of surrender.

"Hold!" Bernard called suddenly.

There was a commotion as raised voices at the gate of the fort guarding the manor drew his attention. Immediately, he leapt to his feet and pulled his own steel sword from its sheath and hurried towards the gate. When he arrived there was a press of people all shouting for the attention of the men watching the gate.

"We need to see the Duke!"

"Yes, take us to see him!"

William took a few deep breaths to recover and then hurried after Bernard, still clutching his wooden sword.

"Wait," Bernard called as he raised his free hand and motioned for the group of villagers outside the gate to hold their silence. "What happened?"

"Bandits, sir," one of the men replied. He clutched a broken arm to his side. "They drove off and scattered the sheep. There was a man with a horrible scar that said the Duke was going to pay for what he did to them. They burned the village and told us to leave." Tears streamed down his face as he spoke of the charred remains of their homes.

Bernard's face was troubled as he motioned for William to step closer, "Go find your father. He is down in the village looking after the folk who arrived last week. Tell him we need him to return to the manor."

"But I want to hear the rest of the story," William protested. He folded his arms and furrowed his brow in protest.

"Go now!" Bernard said as he reached out and cuffed William across the back of the head.

The blow came like lightening and William never saw it coming. He stumbled back as his head rang from the reminder, he should have known better then to talk back to Bernard. He tossed his wooden sword in the corner of the weapons area and jogged away from the manor and down the hill into the village. With the population of the village now over five hundred, he had to search for a while before he found his father watching the progress on a larger dwelling. There were five carpenters placing thick beams across the ceiling and rolls of thatch lying on the ground nearby waiting to be used.

"Father," William called as he skidded to a halt. He glanced at the beams but drew his attention back to his father and the duty he had been asked to perform.

"What is it, Son?" the Duke asked, his eyes strayed towards the manor as if sensing that something was wrong.

"There a bunch of people from Quiet Meadows at the manor," William explained. He turned to follow his father towards the hilltop dwelling. "They said a bandit with a scarred face burned them out and destroyed our sheep."

The Duke kept silent as he considered that day almost ten years ago when he had spared a bandit with a scar on his face. Silently he pondered if the decision had been a rash one. No he thought, it was right. The Savior would not have looked kindly on the death of the unarmed man at the time.

"Are you going to chase him down, Father?" William asked excitedly. His eyes glowed as visions of his father dressed in chain armor riding down hundreds of bandits filled his mind.

"First I am going to see to these people, Son," the Duke replied. "Once I know they are fine I will see about mounting some patrols to watch for the bandits."

"But shouldn't you send soldiers right away?" William asked in disappointment.

"No," Duke Edward replied. "It could be that is what the bandits want us to do. To ride off and leave our homes here poorly defended. We will look to the protection of our people but in our way and time, not on their timing."

"Father?" William asked suddenly as they turned from the cottage.

"What is it son?" the Duke asked quietly. He was tired from the day but still sensed the questions boiling up in his son.

"Why is the Savior letting all these bad things happen to us?" William asked. He didn't understand how someone as faithful as his father could be losing so much in lands and goods.

"Sometimes we cannot see the bigger picture, son," Duke Edward replied. He turned and knelt by William and put his hand on his shoulder. "Sometimes we are looking at things through earthly vision while the Savior is looking down on us with heavenly vision."

William nodded. It was all so hard to understand. He nodded because he wanted to understand but he really didn't. Still, maybe someday he would see it as his father did.

The Duke did not answer further as they walked through the gate and took stock of those gathered inside the walls. There was a clamor of voices as the battered and tired people called for aid and his heart went out to them.

"What will become of us!"

"Can you stop them!"

The Duke held up his hand and motioned for silence, "You are my people and we will find places for you here. Rest assured we will find those who did this and bring them to the king's justice."

The people looked somewhat mollified as the Duke stepped out among them and began to speak with each one personally. Soon the crowd was moving down into the village and men and women from the manor were passing out food and supplies.

William wandered around the village for the rest of the day and finally returned to the manor when the sun was setting. His father was still out and when he finally went to sleep he had still not returned.

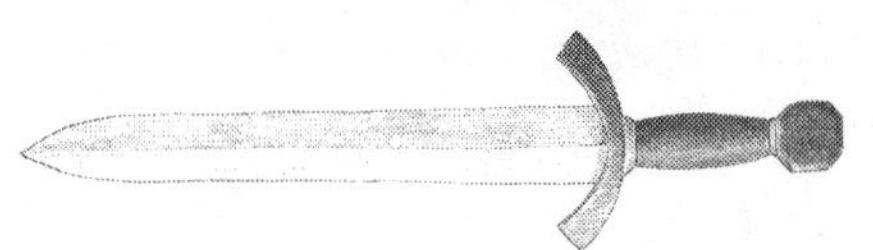

A week passed and this time it was Clair that sought him out. William was sitting on a stone ledge watching a score of workmen as they put the finishing touches on the row of wooden cottages before him. He had spent the morning guiding the horse and wagon back from the woods on the west side of their lands. Another crew was dropping logs and trimming them before cutting the timbers to length and loading them for transport. They were building about three of the cottages per day and at this rate they would have everyone in a snuggly built cottage before the snows began flying.

"William!" Clair called. She waved to him as she walked down the dirt track that connected their lands. "What are you doing?"

"Nothing now," William called back. "I was helping haul timbers but they have enough to finish." He motioned for her to come join him atop the wall but she shook her head.

"Good, come here," Clair said mysteriously. She motioned for him to follow her as she turned and started back down the dirt road. "I have something more fun planned."

William took one last look at the cottage and shrugged. Watching the building go up was fun but he would have much more fun with Clair.

"What's going on?" William asked as they walked side by side. There was a fork in the road and Clair turned to the left instead of using the right track which would have taken her home.

"Remember the old cairns up on Baldtop Peak?" Clair said with a mischievous smile. She reached over and picked up a flower, carefully she slipped it into her thick braid of hair.

William knew the hill she was talking about. Baldtop was many times taller then any other hill in the area and according to Fredrick, it was nearly a mountain. Dotted on the sides near the top on flat sections of the mountain sides were stone tombs covered with grass. Most had been broken open over the years and anything inside them that was worth stealing had been taken by thieves and looters. It was a place of mystery and while not forbidden for him to visit, walking there by himself was frowned on.

"Of course I do," William replied with a shrug.

"The last few weeks there has been light burning on top of Baldtop near dusk," Clair said primly. "I think someone needs to investigate, don't you. Who knows, someone might be in trouble and in need of our help."

Excitement bubbled up inside of William as he thought about a new mystery to examine. "Why, yes I do," William replied. Together they started jogging down the road towards Baldtop. "And since Baldtop is technically on my father's lands I am not even breaking from what he told me to do."

"I told my mom I was coming to visit you," Clair said with a smile. "I am only visiting you where you happen to be. If that is on Baldtop then we are both still obeying."

Baldtop was about an hour walk from the manor and Clair had brought a couple of apples so they munched on the fruit and sipped water from a nearby stream. It was mid-afternoon when they finally started up the first steep trail that would bring them to the top of the mountain. Around them the land was covered with rugged hills and scraggly stands of trees pushing their way up through the thin soil covering the granite under the hills. The one thing that did grow in abundance was the hundreds of wildflowers.

The wind began picking up as they climbed and soon a stiff breeze was pulling at their clothes and making Clair's hair flap wildly.

"Look over there!" William pointed. They were about half way up the mountain when the first of the cairns came into view. All around the tumble of stones was an assortment of tracks, both human and horse.

"Looks like someone pulled a wagon up here at some point," Clair said as she pointed to the deep ruts where a wagon wheel had fallen off the hard packed dirt and slid into the softer ground.

"Why would anyone bring a wagon up here?" William muttered. His thoughts drifted back to the episode in the forest that he had done his best to forget. There were many strange things going on right now, he decided.

They kept climbing and when they reached the mountain side meadow that held the greatest number of cairns, William suddenly grabbed Clair and pushed her off the track and into the taller grass.

"What!" Clair grumbled but then her words froze in her throat. The tumbled remains of a cairn were nearby and they slipped inside the jumble of stones and found shelter.

Scattered about the fairly flat meadows in front of them was almost a score of rough tents. Most of them were simple pieces of hide stretched over wooden frames. There were a few cooking fires still burning from the afternoon meal. Lounging around the tents and close to the fires were clusters of tough looking men. To the west where the grass was thick and green, William saw a rough paddock build to keep their horses from wandering. Filling in one side of the paddock was a line of seven big wagons filled with crates and bags.

"What are they doing?" Clair asked curiously. Her eyes were big as she took in the entire scene before them.

"I don't know," William muttered. "I have never seen any of these men before." His own brow furrowed together as he tried to decide in his mind what was going on here.

"Neither have I," Clair muttered. "We have to tell someone this time." She looked at him with pleading eyes.

"I agree this is too important this time, something is going on and my father needs to know," William said as they crawled on all fours back down the trail. They hurried down the trail for several hundred yards and then rose to their feet. William leaned over to brush the dirt from his pants and when he looked up and spoke he stumbled to a halt.

Standing in front of them was a man with a straggly beard on his face and a tunic that was covered in dirt. More importantly, he was carrying the carcass of deer thrown over one shoulder, a quiver of arrows, and a long bow in other hand.

"What the," the man exclaimed. He started to drop the deer and reach for an arrow but William was quicker.

With a lightning fast leap forward he shoved the man as hard as he could. "Run Clair!" he shouted. The man's arms windmilled for a moment and then he tumbled backwards over the lip of a small rise and his head clucked against a stone. The remains of the deer flopped down on top of him burying him under its weight. The man laid silently under the weight of the deer, his breath coming in slow gasps.

All was silent for a moment as Clair stared at William and he stared at the half unconscious man who lay groaning on the ground staring at the grass. The deer stared off into space and William thought for one second it probably wondered what they were all waiting on.

"RUN!" William said loudly again.

William and Clair bolted as fast as

their legs would carry them down the mountain trail as above them on the mountain they heard a confused shout. The walk to Baldtop which had taken them an hour was over in less then a third of that time.

When they finally arrived back at the village, both of them were panting wildly and the work men who had just finished putting the roof in place looked at them curiously.

"What happened to you two?" Bernard said as he walked around the corner and looked at their red faces.

"Bernard, I promise I didn't leave our lands!" William erupted and then he froze realizing he had just given away their recent escapade.

"What happened William?" Bernard asked as his eyes narrowed. "Tell me now."

"We just went to go see the view from Baldtop Mountain," Clair said as tears filled her eyes. "We never got in trouble for hiking up there before."

The story came in a jumbled heap of words and once Bernard had it sorted he shook his head. "Both of you head up to the manor. I need to round up some men and go look into this." With that he turned and trotted off into the village leaving them both crestfallen and scared that they were going to be punished again.

"Did you find anything?"

William was sitting at the table with Bernard and his father trying hard to shrink out of sight into his chair.

"Nothing, sire, but the remains of a fairly large campsite that had been used for at most a few days." Bernard reported in a solemn voice. "What are these men up to? It did look like they have been hauling heavily loaded wagons up there for some time now."

"I wish I knew, Bernard," the Duke replied thoughtfully. "Whatever it is, each time we come close to them they vanish for a season before reappearing. They must have a base of operations nearby that we have not found."

"Black Bier Estate," William burst out not able to contain himself any longer. "It has to be Father."

"While this time I tend to agree with you son, we cannot simply move our soldiers into our neighbors lands without more proof." The Duke tapped his chin thoughtfully. "Better see to the training of as many men as we can Bernard and let Baron Corduval know so that he can see to his own defenses."

"Yes, sire," Bernard replied.

"We are a long ways from the throne here on the edge of the Wilds and we must be prepared," the Duke said. "We have known peace for a long time but it seems that we must now look to our borders and prepare our defenses."

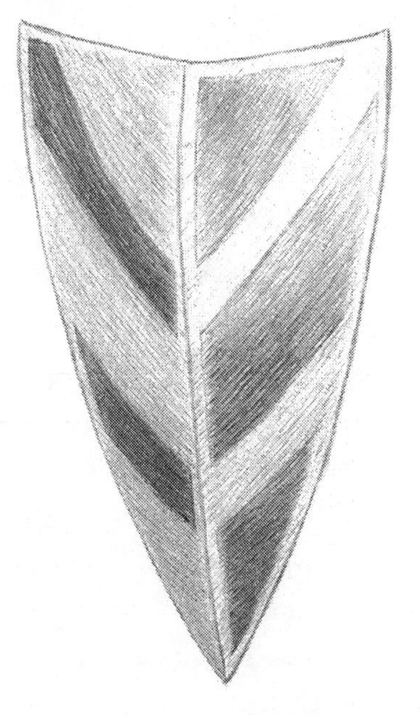

7 – Conrad's Sneer

The rest of the summer passed by quietly with many patrols scouting around the north and west sections of the Duke's lands but finding little. William managed to be present for most of the reports brought in by tired scouts and each time it was the same. No one had seen anything. They brought news though, that the mysterious and not so friendly knight from the Old Mill Pond manor had been seen riding along the borders of their lands. He had also established a series of outposts and had men watching the border that looked less than honorable. Still the days passed by quietly and no movement was seen from the watchers.

It was early fall and the harvest had been plentiful. William had finally been freed back to just his normal chores and things seemed to have settled into a peaceful rhythm as preparations for winter took place. With almost a hundred and fifty more people in the village, several new streets now stretched out into the distance from the Manor and four new storage barns now dominated the sky to the east of the village.

That morning William rose and went to the practice yard after eating a quick breakfast. After an hour of working with his sword, he walked back around to the front of the manor and immediately noticed the saddled horses.

"What's going on?" William asked. He noted that there were nearly fifty horses and a great knot of men wearing chain armor standing quietly before the gate. The tension in the air was thick and he felt his own pulse quicken.

"The Duke is leading us towards Rock Downs," one of the men replied. "One of the scouts brought word that strange men were seen scouting the area last night just after the moon crested in the sky."

William's heart began pounding when

he saw Conrad standing by his mount with his chest puffed out. When William looked over at him he stuck out his tongue, when no one was looking, and sneered at him.

"Not fair," William muttered under his breath. Immediately he looked around and spotted his father standing with Bernard and speaking in low tones. He ran as fast as he could to where they were standing and skidded to a halt.

"Father, I want to go with you!" William burst out.

"No, Son," the Duke said calmly.

"But Conrad gets to go. I want to go," William protested. "I am getting as good with the bow as he is…"

"No Son," the Duke repeated as he put his hand on William's shoulder. "You are not ready for this yet, remember all things must happen in His timing not ours."

"I agree with the Duke," Bernard said. He nodded down to William, "You are progressing well but you are not ready for this yet. Stay here and keep watch on the townsfolk." With that settled he turned back to Duke Edward and continued discussing how to proceed.

William frowned so furiously that he

thought his face was going to break. Moisture welled up in his eyes but he fought it back as disappointment filled him.

"Mount up," the Duke called. He swung his leg over the back of his tall warhorse and looked down at William. "Watch over your mother until I return."

As the column of men rode out Conrad was near the end and he leaned over and laughed at William, "Yes, do watch over the chickens also while we are out." With that he urged his mount on and caught up with the rest of the force.

William turned away without answering and stomped off towards the manor. When he heard the horses start away down the road north he fled as fast as his feet could carry him.

He ran north into a thick stand of trees and then entered a small lane that wandered through the fields but closely mirrored the large dirt track where his father rode. He wanted to see what was going to happen and if he was forced to run all the way there he would.

Rebellion and anger filled him, why should his brother get to go along with the force and he be left at home. Still, his father had told him to stay at home and, even as he ran, a small bit of remorse for deciding to disobey his father filled him and urged him to return home. He pushed back the feeling and kept running. He just wanted to see what was going to happen after all. There was no harm in that, was there?

He was halfway to the edge of their lands when he was finally forced to stop, to try and catch his breath. In the distance there was cloud of dust moving towards him so he started up a nearby tree. When he was cleverly hidden in the leafy heights he watched. From his vantage point, he could see his father's force moving north in the distance but it seemed to have shrunk in his estimation. He scanned to where the other bit of dust was hanging in the air and suddenly spotted something out of place. There was a shallow depression in the ground and a few downed trees for cover. Hidden there was a separate group of men on foot crouched behind a hill west of his father's men. From the tree top he saw them easily and understood that as his father was chasing one group, another was getting ready to attack.

The bandits were crouched down and trying to remain out of sight and there was a lookout watching the approach of the Duke's force.

Even though staying hidden was the smarter of his choices, considering he had no weapons, William slipped back down the tree and bolted across the field towards where his father was approaching. *This would do it* he thought. *He would warn his father and save the day*.

He heard a scuffle of footsteps to his right and turned his head just in time to see a man in dirty clothes reach out and cuff him hard. William rolled head over heels across the freshly harvested field and bits of stalks poked into his skin each time. When he finally came to a halt it was with a crash against the stump of a tree that left him stunned.

He staggered as he got back to his feet and tried to continue running towards his father's force. The world spun wildly around him and he staggered forward as his legs refused to respond to his mind.

"Father!" He started to shout but a rough pair of hands grabbed him and a smelly set of fingers was clamped over his face.

"Where did the brat come from?"

"I don't know but he about gave us away," replied the man holding William tightly against his chest.

"Tie him up and put him over there," the first bandit replied. "The Duke is almost in position. Scar Face will not be happy if his plan is interrupted."

William felt rope being wrapped around his wrists and he knew he had one last chance to warn his father. He struggled wildly and finally wiggled around until his teeth were in line with one of the dirty fingers and then he chomped down as hard as he could. The grip on him released almost at once as the man yelped in pain and dropped him to the ground. He scrambled to his feet and lunged away from the press of bandits.

"Grab him!" Someone shouted.

William bolted to the right trying to clear the depression but there was a gathering of startled faces looking back at him from that side so he cut back to the left. There was a down tree on that side and he managed to wiggle under it. Pumping his legs furiously he managed to reach the summit of the depression in the ground just as his father and his small force appeared.

"William!" the Duke cried out then he

motioned him men forward. "Look out!"

Suddenly, there was another figure off to his right and he was swinging a thick club with a heavy weight of iron on the end.

A hard sharp blow struck his right arm and the sound of a bone breaking echoed across the field. William felt an intense pain lance through his body and then he was flying into the ground again as shouts filled the air.

From where he lay off to the side, William saw his father's men charge across the field. They were outnumbered three to one but they had better training and were mounted. They swung the swords with precision as they battled the group of bandits that boiled out of their hiding place.

"Ohh," William muttered as he struggled to push his body up with his left arm. As he looked up there was a second rush of men from the north that crashed into the Duke force and began driving them back. Scattered across the field, he could see the bodies of the bandits and here and there were a few of his father's men. Then there was a third shout and the twang of a score of bows as the missing half of his father's men erupted from hiding and loosed a deadly flight of arrows at the new comers. Four fell from their saddles immediately and the others were caught between continuing their head long attack at the beleaguered Duke and turning towards the hidden archers.

Four more bandits slipped from their saddles before the rest broke and fled north. When those on the ground saw that the ambush had failed and that their fellows were fleeing, they too turned tail and ran as fast as they could for the denser forests to the north where they could lose the Duke's men in the trees.

"Son, what are you doing here?" the Duke asked quietly when he pulled his warhorse to a halt and dismounted. Carefully he picked up William in his strong arms and carried him over to where his men were gathering.

"Check the dead for anything that gives a clue as to who leads them or where they are coming from," the Duke ordered.

"What of the boy?" Bernard asked as he shook his head. "Looks like his arm is broken."

"Yes, it is, and it will have to be set in place and bound tightly," The Duke replied.

Bernard grimaced as he looked at the

broken limb and shook his head, "He should have stayed home."

"This is going to hurt son," the Duke said gently. His eyes were sad as he looked down at William.

"I am sorry, Father..." William was about to reply when a horrible wave of pain shot through his arm and black spots filled his eyes.

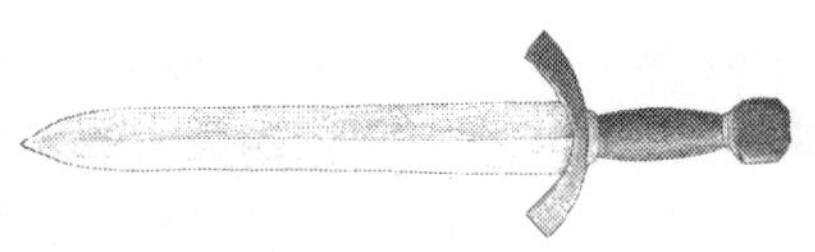

The Duke pulled as gently as he could on the broken bone and felt it with his fingers. Thankfully, his son passed out almost immediately and he was able to bring the two halves of the bone together and set them in place. The break was a clean one and he set two small splints in place around the arm and bound them with strips of clean cloth.

When he was done setting the broken arm, he climbed back into his saddle and took William in his arms.

"We will ride back to the manor," the Duke said to Bernard. "Finish cleaning up the fallen and bring what you find back when you are done."

"It will be done, sire," Bernard replied.

He motioned for two men who were standing nearby. "Escort the Duke and his son back to the manor."

Bernard turned back to his work as the Duke rode away. He could see a familiar figure approaching from where the archers were climbing out of their ambush spot. The battle had been carefully organized to bring victory with the least amount of lost life.

"Was that my brother?" Conrad asked as he approached. Bits of leaves and grass were still stuck to his armor and excitement shown in his eyes.

"Yes, he disobeyed your father and tried to watch what was happening, He nearly lost his life for his foolishness," Bernard replied. He gave Conrad a hard look as he tried to decide if the older boy had done anything to make the situation worse. "You didn't know anything about it, did you?"

"I don't know anything," he said sullenly. Conrad shook his head, his hands were still shaking with the excitement and a bit of fear that he felt. This had been his first battle against bandits and he had failed to even make one shot count.

"I missed every shot I took," Conrad muttered as he looked down at where the still figures of the bandits were being gathered. Most wore simple pieces of leather armor and their faces were smudged and dirty. There were twelve total that had fallen and three of Duke Edwards's men had given their lives.

"It is that way many times," Bernard said with a sad smile. "On the other hand though if you get too good at fighting and it fails to make you at least a little scared, it is time for you to step back and remember what is truly important."

Conrad nodded.

"Come, let us examine our bandits and see if there is anything that we can learn from their appearance and equipment," Bernard said. He motioned for Conrad to follow him and they walked to where the twelve bandits who had not survived the attack were laid out in an even row.

As he looked down at the faces of the dead men, Bernard felt a sense of great sadness come over him. Here were men who had chosen a path that ended their lives early and they would never be able to hear the wonderful story of what the Savior had done for them.

"What a wasted life," Conrad muttered. He watched as Bernard knelt down and looked closely at the material that the bandit's shirt was made of.

"Look here," Bernard said to Conrad as he flipped the inside of the material over for him to see. "This material is not made anywhere around here. Indeed, I would be surprised if it was made in any of the nations near our shores. It comes from far away."

"Where is it from?" Conrad asked as he looked at the fine weave of the material. It was not at all what one would expect from a group of vagabond criminals.

"The only place I have ever seen this type of weave is when I was in the Holy Land," Bernard replied. "And look at this dagger." He took the knife from the small leather sheath and handed it to Conrad.

The older boy looked at the steel and could see the many lines of quality Damashalta steel worked into the blade.

"This dagger is made of the finest quality steel but it is covered in mud as though there is something that they wished to hide from anyone who might be watching," Bernard said. He looked up at the boy to see if his mind was working on the problem. "What does this tell us?"

Conrad turned the blade over in his

hand. Finally, he looked Bernard and said, "That someone very powerful and with connections to the Holy Land is trying to ruin my family?" His statement ended in a question.

"Do you know of anyone who fits this description?" Bernard asked. He knew the Duke had been involved in the Second Crusade also but there were many mysteries surrounding him.

"I do not, maybe my father does," Conrad replied. He grunted, "And my brother almost gave the entire thing away didn't he?"

"He came close," Bernard agreed.

8 – *Fire!*

William regained his senses sometime later and he looked up to see his father's worried face looking down at him.

"I am sorry, Father," William said as tears filled his eyes. "I don't know why I did it. I want to obey but sometimes I just can't seem to control myself."

"It's alright, Son," the Duke said. "I just wanted to keep you out of harm's way."

"Those men were going to ambush you," William said, as he wiped away the tears with his left hand. His right arm throbbed wildly but he gritted his teeth and shrugged away the pain as best he could.

"I know that, Son," the Duke replied. "Bernard's men spotted them soon after we left the manor and we split our force to deal with them."

William shook head as he realized that his father had known about the ambush from the start. In fact, he had nearly alerted the bandits to the presence of his father's men as they eluded the ambush and arranged an ambush of their own.

"Sleep now, Son," the Duke said. "All is safe for now."

William was drowsy anyway and he nodded. The throbbing in his arm was going away and the limb simply felt numb now. As he drifted off to sleep he heard Conrad return and begin talking to his father but he was too tired to follow what was being said.

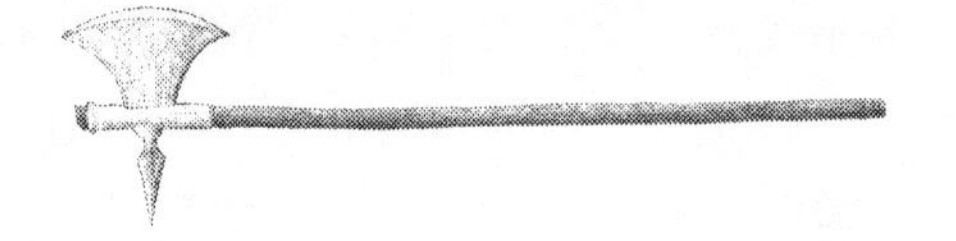

"We found nothing that gave away who they work for, Father," Conrad said as he stood in the hallway near William's bed. "They were carrying blades like these." He handed the knife to his father and pointed to the quality of the steel. "And their clothes were of fine cuts of cloth, not like I would think bandits would be wearing."

"I agree with you, Son," the Duke

replied. "These are not ordinary bandits. They have been sent here for a purpose.

"Why, Father?" Conrad asked curiously.

"I cannot tell you yet, Son," the Duke said quietly. "When the time is right, then you will know." The Duke turned away from his son and walked back down the halls to where Bernard was sitting at the long table sipping on a tankard of water and resting from the day.

"Did you send out more scouts?" the Duke asked.

"Yes," Bernard replied. "I can tell you what they will say. The tracks lead north into the area around the old mill town and then they will be turned back by our mysterious neighbor."

"Suggestions?" the Duke asked curiously. He had an idea of how to proceed but he learned long ago to trust Bernard's instincts and to listen to the advice he offered.

"We should increase our forces by another fifty," Bernard said without hesitation. "And establish hidden places to keep watch on the northern edges of your lands. Your brothers of The Order might have angered the might of the heathens or whatever is taking place could have its roots closer to home. We must be watchful and above all try and find this bandit with the scared face who leads them."

"Cut off the head of the snake and the body will die," the Duke said with a nod. "Work on finding us the recruits and begin their training."

"It will cost you many coins," Bernard pointed out as he rose to his feet.

"Lay up not earthly treasures," the Duke said with a smile. "Send at least twenty men to guard Calavort. I do not want all of the villages that we have worked so hard to establish on our lands destroyed."

Bernard nodded, he agreed with the decision but it would leave them dangerously undermanned here at the manor until he could find, recruit, and train more men.

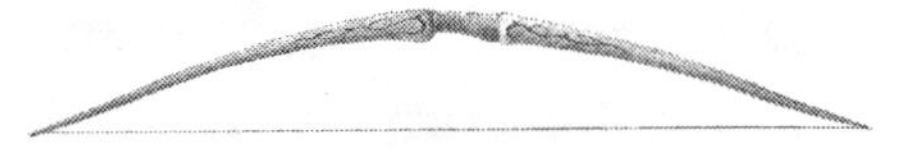

The rest of the fall passed by quietly and William's arm healed slowly. Soon it was the deepest part of the winter and tempers in the manor grew short. Even worse the Duke had to take advantage of the single break in the weather and rode south to speak with a man about goods that he had purchased and was gone for a time.

William was stuck doing odd chores around the manor that he could handle with his left arm. Conrad seemed distant and when Father was not looking he sneered at William.

"Knock it off," William said one day about a week after his fifteenth birthday. He was not wearing his splint anymore but his mother and father still would not let him back into the weapons practice area.

"You almost cost us the entire battle that day," Conrad erupted finally. He had been seething about the events from last fall until now and he finally spoke his mind.

"Bernard said that you almost got us all killed," Conrad continued as he pointed his finger at his brother. "When are you going to stop acting like a spoiled little brat?"

William shouted back at him and a moment later he launched his body across the table and tried to hit Conrad in the face. There was a quick jab from Conrad and suddenly a burst of stars erupted before his eyes.

"Knock it off you two!" Bernard shouted as he entered the room and cuffed Conrad across the back of the head. He grabbed William and hauled him back by the scruff of his shirt. "Your father is gone for less than a week on his annual trip and you two are at each other's throats."

"I hate you!" William shouted at Conrad. He struggled in Bernard's iron grip but could not break free.

"I hate you too," Conrad muttered back at him as he turned and stomped off towards his room on the second floor. He went up the steps and slammed the door to his room loudly.

"Stop struggling William," Bernard said as he pulled the boy back and slapped him down in a chair. "Now then, what is all this about?"

"He said I almost got everyone killed," William said as he fought back the tears in his eyes. "It's not true, is it?"

"No boy, it's not true," Bernard replied. "It was a little worrisome when we were forced to stop our attack and rescue you but it all worked out fine."

William was aghast, in so many words Bernard had just admitted that he nearly killed them. Deep inside, the news made him all the angrier with his brother and he turned and fled to his own room.

Four days later, William was out helping clear the fresh layer of snow from the road leading to the manor when suddenly there was a shout of surprise. He paused with a full load of snow in his rough shovel and looked around to find who was shouting the warnings.

"Sire," a breathless villager shouted as he struggled through the knee deep snow towards them. The white layer was thick and heavy and clearing it was taking forever.

"What is it?" Conrad called from where he stood. He held his own shovel piled with snow.

"Trouble at the Corduval Estate sire," the man called.

Williams's heart beat fast in his chest. He had spent many days over the last summer and fall with Clair. If something was happening at their manor he needed to know, he threw down his shovel and thrashed through the snow until he reached the shelter of the village. Many of the roads were already clear and he was able to run with his head down until he reached the road leading south. As he rounded the last cottage, he skidded to a halt and stared in horror. Great flames erupted from each of the windows of the distant manor and rolls of black smoke lifted skyward.

"We have to go help them," William cried out as his brother skidded to a halt next to him. He grabbed Conrad's arm and pulled on him.

"How, the road is closed with snow," Conrad said quietly. "We can't clear it in time."

This time William's heart sank low in his chest. He knew his brother was right but he hated him for saying it. The road had not been cleared all winter and the snow was piled waist high in places.

"We can at least clear the way so that we can send help," Bernard's rigid voice spoke from behind them. He motioned the people around him forward. "Go gather everyone from the village. We have much work to do."

William despaired as he watched the people around him attack the drifts. Their shovels seemed so puny against the amount of snow that the winter had dumped on them this far. Drifts as high as a man's chest blocked their path and more fell slowly even as they tried to clear a way.

The rest of the day was spent taking turns shoveling and when night fell and the temperature dropped Bernard had the people light torches and fires. Working by the flickering lights, they pushed on until by midnight they had passed the chapel. Still, that only put them a little over halfway. The fire in the manor burned hard for many hours and then slowly faded until nothing remained of the inner building but a blackened husk. The outer walls were stone but the wooden roof was gone and the fire leapt once into one of the great storage barns raised just the year before.

It was noon the next day when the exhausted people led by Bernard broke through the last of the snow banks. The village around the Corduval estate was alive with activity and smiles of relief filled faces as two great wagons filled with food rumbled into the land before the ruined manor.

"What happened?" Bernard asked as Baron Corduval wiped the layer of tears from his eyes and brushed away the ones sticking to his beard.

"I don't know. The fire started in the

middle of the night," the Baron responded. "My men are checking the area around the manor for tracks but it started in an outside wall. I would say it was set by someone deliberately."

"Where is Clair?" William burst out. His heart beat a sigh of relief when he saw the bedraggled form of Clair emerge from a nearby cottage. Then he realized that he had not seen Charles yet. "Where is Charles?"

There was a fresh round of tears from the baron and he covered his face with his hand.

Williams's heart fell as he saw the same tears of anguish on Clair's face. Something horrible had happened to his friend and his own heart sank to his feet.

"Charles didn't make it out," the Baron finally managed to say. "He helped me get Clair and his mother out and then he went back in to help one of our men get his son out. The roof collapsed before they could get out."

William stared in horror at the still smoking remains of the great manor house. He was exhausted from lack of sleep and the thought of his friend dying in the horrible fire was almost too much for him to comprehend.

They spent the rest of the day bringing supplies from their own storage barns over to the village surrounding the Corduval Manor and by that evening were able to return home.

William was sitting at the table half asleep when Bernard entered and shook the snow from his hair and shoulders.

"Did you find anything?" William's mother asked quietly. With her husband due back any day now, she was ready to sit back again and let him return to the serious work of running the manor.

"Yes ma'am," Bernard replied in low tone. "Someone tried to fire our supply barns last night also but the snow put the fire out. We were lucky last night."

"Luck had nothing to do with it," the Lady of the manor replied. "The Savior gave us a chance to survive so that we could bless our neighbors."

Bernard nodded.

"Double the watch," she said. "I sense someone is trying to weaken us for something big. There are many people who live in the Wilds that disagree with the King and envy those of us who live in the King's Land. We may be facing something greater then just winter storms."

9 – A Crusade

The rest of the winter went by quietly and it was late spring when William ventured north again. He was helping prepare the fields for planting and they were working on a field that bordered the mysterious knight's lands.

William scurried up the nearest tree when they arrived at the field and the first thing he saw was a solitary figure watching them.

"He is just sitting there watching us," William said to Bernard who arrived about an hour later. The runner who had gone to warn the soldier sat panting nearby.

"It is alright," Bernard said as he looked towards the distant dark figure sitting on his warhorse. "You go ahead and get started on the field while we keep watch." Ten men had come with him and motioned his men to spread out and keep watch on the distant tree line. The dark figure of the knight and his horse was stationed on a hilltop just outside of the stand of trees and he had not moved in nearly an hour and half.

William walked out into the field and this time he opted to keep his boots on. It would be hard work later to clean the spring mud from the boots but he wanted to be able to run if he needed to.

They worked for the entire morning while the knight watched and suddenly near midday he turned his horse and vanished into the trees.

"What a strange man," William said as they gathered up their belongings. They finished with this field and were beginning to work their way back towards the manor.

It was a week later when the rider arrived wearing the livery of the king and escorted by two men wearing heavy chain armor. A fourth man in robes rode with them but his cloak was pulled high and William could see nothing of his face. The messenger carried a wooden scroll case and he passed it to Duke Edward with a bow.

"A message from the King, sire," the rider said.

"How is King Alalion?" Duke Edward asked.

"King Alalion died this winter sire," the rider replied with a sad face. "His son Targo rules now with the aid of the Grand Bishop Arod."

A dark cloud covered the Duke's face as he opened the missive and read it carefully. When he was done reading he shook his head.

"A third crusade?" Duke Edward asked quietly. "Why?"

"I do not know," the rider said. "I do know that the kings of Fregland and the Emperor of Barbadu have pledged men and supplies. Word is that their armies will be ready to march sometime next year."

"I will not answer this call," Duke Edward said firmly. There was no hint of compromise in his voice.

William stared curiously at his dad as he noticed the change come over him. He had not seen his father back away from a call by the king but this time was different. The face of the messenger showed that he disapproved of Duke Edward's decision but he was only delivering the parchment.

Suddenly the robed man pushed his mount forward and leaned over the duke slightly. William noticed that Bernard's hand went to his sword immediately and moments later so did the two soldiers escorting the rider. The tension in the air rose quickly as the soldiers glared at each other.

"You would defy an order from your rightful king," the robed man said in an oily voice. "Have you forgotten who granted you these lands and title?"

William shuddered slightly as the voice reminded him a snake's hiss.

"No, I have not forgotten," Duke Edward replied. He motioned for Bernard to step back. "I still keep the king's decree that says these lands belong to my family for services rendered during the last crusade. I was there and saw what the men of the cloth and their servants did to those who surrendered. My protests were drowned out by the shouts of those around me who cried for blood."

William stared at his father in amazement. He had never heard his father talk about what had happened during the war.

"The Holy City that you helped free was taken again last year by the infidels," the robed man continued. "Would you leave it in their hands?"

"What is more important? A city that has fallen into disrepair or a man's soul," Duke Edward responded. "Give them the words of the Savior if you wish to change them. But I will not send my people to be slaughtered at the gates or to kill the souls we should be saving."

"Is that your final decision?" the robed man asked. He sat back up straight in his saddle and held his head high. Still his face was hidden in the depths of his hooded robe.

"It is," Duke Edward replied firmly.

"Sad," the robed figure responded. "And just when I could have helped you with your bandit problem."

There was almost a minute of silence where both parties glared at each other but finally the messenger spoke. "If you notice, at the bottom of the missive, that those who wish to forego sending soldiers to fight will be charged a support tax. This is required by the crown so that troops can be hired in your place. The cost for you, Duke Edward, and your manor is smaller since your lands are small. One hundred pieces of gold will be due at the end of year when your tribute is given to the crown. Of course, the army will not march for almost a year and half while supplies are stored and weapons prepared. If in that time you change your mind the crown can be most generous."

There was a round of startled gasps and even William understood that one hundred pieces of gold was a heavy price for a small manor. His father simply nodded his head meekly and William wondered what had happened to the man that had charged fearlessly into battle with bandits to save his life.

The robed man and the others turned their mounts to leave and William finally caught a glimpse of the man's face. He was young but with a pointed black beard covering much of his face. He smiled wickedly at William as they trotted their mounts down the road towards Baron Corduval's estate.

"Father?" William started but his

father's look cut him short.

"Not now, Son," Duke Edward replied. He motioned for Bernard to follow him and walked towards the keep leaving a growing roar of conversation in his trail.

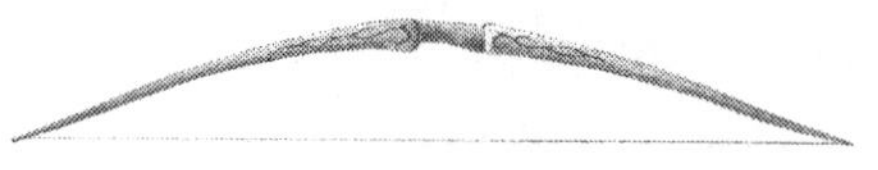

It was the beginning of the summer and several weeks had passed since the news of the Third Crusade had arrived at their lands. William was now fifteen and nearly as tall as his father. With Conrad now considered a man at eighteen it fell to William to do many of the things that Conrad had done before. This was how he found himself making the trip to Fredrick's to pick up a dozen bows for his father. Along with the thirty pieces of gold was a list of weapons that had to be sent within the next year's time to the City of the King.

"William," Fredrick said with a wide smile when he saw him coming up the path.

"How are you?" William responded. He was leading a mare hooked to a small wagon loaded with supplies for making arrows. They unloaded in silence and when the new bows were packed carefully in to the wagon, William sat down with Fredrick for lunch. He always enjoyed sitting in the cottage with the smell of spices heavy in the air.

"Why will Father not go on the crusade," William asked Fredrick curiously. "What is he scared of? If the church is behind it doesn't that mean it is the will of the Savior?"

Fredrick stopped and looked at him. The knife he was using to cut up carrots taken from the storage area beneath the cottage stopped in mid air.

"Has another crusade been called?" Fredrick asked curiously.

"Yes," William said a bit proudly. Even with his father's words ringing in his mind he still felt the excitement of the moment and the want to drive the blood thirsty infidels from lands that did not belong to them and restore western control to the Holy City.

"That is a long story," Fredrick said as he finished slicing the carrot and dropped it into the iron pot.

"I have time," William said hopefully.

"Alright then," Fredrick said. "But I am going to prepare my supper while I tell it." He continued gathering herbs and spices, slowly adding pinches of each to the pot until he seemed happy with the result.

He was silent for such a long time that William thought maybe he had changed his mind but then he began telling the story.

"It was winter almost sixteen years ago when word arrived that the church was raising an army to take back the Holy City. I know," Fredrick raised his hand as questions erupted in Williams eyes. "Your father followed the old priests' words and never questioned a thing. Despite your mother's misgivings, he and Bernard took up the call and went south to the City of the King and joined the expedition. I met him there, I was traveling and my expertise with making bows was well known so I was hired to make bows as quickly as I could for the coming war. Now understand this situation was not new, the Infidels took control of the Holy Land nearly seventy years ago. However, two years before the crusade a new Grand Bishop was elected and word began to filter out of atrocities committed against pilgrims who went to visit the Holy City. Of course, none of us ever spoke to anyone who had witnessed any of these things but we believed what we were told and anger filled us. We were ready for war and happy to board the ships. All told, seventeen thousand marched from Britoria and landed in Pagali in my own homeland of Fregland. There the king of my homeland added fifteen thousand to our ranks and we marched the divide in the Torva Mountains and into church lands. By the time we reached the port city of Rummu, we had close to fifty thousands soldiers."

Fredrick puttered with the iron pot for a couple more moments and then hung it on the hook above the fire and added a couple of small logs. When he was happy that the soup would survive on its own for a time, he sat down across from William and continued.

"Now keep in mind the First Crusade was a success and the Holy City was free of infidels for nearly fifty years before it fell again. However things had been peaceful and free travel was allowed so no one cared."

Fredrick fell silent again for a moment and tears appeared in his eyes as he finally continued telling the story.

"It was a short journey by ship to round the edge of the Grimal Mountains. You can't go by land because the mountains erupted straight out of the Sea of Tears and travel by land force a large for is impossible.

The Isle of Jut was taken as a staging area and then we made land just south of the mountains and began our march. It was here that your father and Bernard first began to have misgivings. The Infidels that met us were not the uncultured savages that we had expected. Indeed, when they saw the strength that marched with us many tried to surrender but the priests ordered that no quarter be given. The slaughter that day was horrible, and not even those who lived in the Holy Land before the Infidels took it were spared."

William was shocked to hear this but at the same time the images of the grand battles filled his mind. Oh, he thought, to be a part of something that big and splendid.

"After that the Infidels attacked us almost daily and each day we lost more and more men. They fought from horseback but were lightly armored. They managed to slow our march to a crawl and finally, within sight of the Holy City, we were met by an army that matched ours in size and strength. There the kings came together and signed a treaty with the leader of the Infidels. The island of Jut was left in our hands and a small triangle of land just south of the Grimal Mountains to act as a loading port for pilgrims. Then we left," Fredrick finished. He looked closely at William and realized the boy was still staring out into the air beyond him dreamily.

"William!" Fredrick said. "William, it was not a good thing what we did. We should have listened to men like your father who told us to bring the Holy Word to the Infidels and preach the Savior to them."

"Oh, that doesn't sound exciting," William said dreamily as he shook his head. "I need to get going."

William left the small cottage and the gardens with a spring in his step. The Crusade didn't leave for another year. By that time he would be eighteen and able to make his own decisions. He would go fight for the church and gain the glory that he deserved. With those thoughts swirling in his mind, he started down the trail towards the manor. Overhead the sun began to slowly dip towards the horizon and he failed to see the shadowy figures that entered the meadows and started towards Fredrick's cottage.

10 – Fredrick's Plight

William heard the shouts of panic behind him and his blood froze in his veins. He grabbed a bow from the cart behind him and a full quiver of arrows and sprinted back up the trail towards Fredrick's cottage.

When he arrived at the edge of the wood he dove for cover behind the massive trunk of a tree and looked around the trunk. Almost a score of men stood around the cottage as it burned brilliantly and sparks floated up into the air.

"Fredrick," William said in a panic. Then his mind calmed as he saw the old Freglander standing in the middle of a group of bandits with his hands securely tied behind his back.

As he watched, the men laughed and carried on as they ran their mounts across the carefully arranged gardens scattered around the meadow and ground the herbs and spices into the ground.

"Come, old man," one of the bandits said with a laugh. "Our master has need of a new Fletcher and Black Brier Estate is your new home now."

This is it William thought to himself, *I can finally prove to my father that I am a man*. I will rescue Fredrick and bring him back to our manor. He withdrew an arrow from his quiver and waited in the deepest of the shadows while the bandits finished their sport and began to filter out of the clearing.

"We need to move," one of the men finally called out to his brethren.

"Yes, Scar Face and the others are waiting for us."

"The big boss isn't gonna be happy when he finds out what Scar is up to," another one laughed. Despite the chuckle he seemed a bit nervous to William who wondered just who this person was who was pulling the strings of this group.

"Let's move! This is the one night that he will be away from his home. Its time to pay his place a visit and see if we can leave the home fires burning for him."

William was not sure what they were talking about but he was happy to hear them finally give the order to leave the meadow. He nearly fainted when the group turned towards his hiding place. He shrank into the deepest corner of the small depression in the trunk of the tree and closed his eyes. He hoped they were so night blinded from staring into the fire that they would miss him and thankfully he turned out to be right.

Four of the men walked right by him laughing and never even paused.

Where are they going? William thought to himself. When the coast was clear he stepped out and followed the group. They kept to the trail that led them deeper into his father lands and seemed on a course that would take them straight to his father's manor house.

William started running as fast as his legs could carry him. His father and Bernard were away to the south at the edge of Hardarva's Wall arranging the purchase of enough sheep to replace the stolen ones. They had taken a score of soldiers with them. With those men away. the contingent that remained at the manor was ill equipped to deal with an outright attack.

Still, William thought as he ran. He cut to the left leaving the main trail and taking a smaller game trail that would put him ahead of the bandits. Off to his right he could see the single torch that one of the men carried to light their path and he was leaving them behind. How could they know that the manor was unguarded, the gruff man's voice came echoing back to him, unless there was a spy somewhere in the village that his father did not know about.

Panic set into William but he forced himself to breath through it like Bernard had taught him and slowly his mind calmed. The first thing he would do is see about trying to find the turncoat. Then he would race ahead of the bandits and warn the village.

The bandits were still about a half a league to his right so he leapt over the fence and started across the field separating them. He could still see the single torch but he assumed that they would extinguish it the moment they were within sight of the manor walls.

"Where are you," William muttered as he skidded to a halt behind a low section of the stone wall. The bandits had come to an intersection of two trails and were now waiting. If they turned to the right they would reach the remains of Quiet Meadows waiting to be rebuilt. If they continued south they would reach his father's manor and the larger village.

Still, they would need more men if they thought they would take the manor and the village, William thought to himself.

"Here he comes now," said a gruff voice. William dared to raise his head over the wall. He could see a dark figure slinking along the trail in darkness.

Suddenly something occurred to William, he set his bow and quiver off to the side and got down and rolled in the softer and wetter dirt near the wall. Then he took his hands off took his weapons and slipped over the wall at the back of the bandit group.

"What happened to you?" a man waiting at the back of the group said curiously.

"Made a wrong turn after we left the old man's house and ended up in the middle of that field. Slipped when I was coming to meet up with you," William muttered in his roughest voice. He looked down at the mud covering him and shrugged, "What can you do?" he asked with a shake of his head.

The other man laughed quietly and slapped him on the shoulder, "I can't wait to make these rich brats pay. Soon those of us who live in the Wilds will have a place at the kings table."

"It's about time too," William muttered.

"Aye," the man agreed. "Why should we be kept out."

William nodded as he listened to the man talk. Finally he pointed up to where the shadowy figure had just arrived and spoke.

"What's his story?"

"Who, the spy?" the man said with a laugh. "Oh we have many of them spread out throughout the northern estates. The cleanest and most well spoken of those in our ranks are chosen to go live among the King's people and keep us informed of what is happening. We never really made much use of them until Scar Face returned."

"I heard he was in the King's Dungeon for a while," William ventured. "I wonder what that was like."

"I don't rightly know," the man replied.

The bandit seemed to want to talk so William ventured a little closer to the meeting happening on the road while he listened. The rest of the bandits were lounging around the stone walls and none seemed to be paying any attention.

"All this talk of the Savior and the church," the man grunted quietly. "It's enough to make your stomach turn. I, for one, will not have anyone telling me what to do. We are all free spirits: take what we want from the richer lands, take the things we deserve, and go back to our dens in the Wilds."

William noticed that the man's voice was fading and he glanced back to see him sitting on the fence still talking even though no one was now listening.

"I tell you the lord of the manor is away to the south buying sheep," the shadow said quietly. "I asked at the manor to speak to him today and they said he would be back tomorrow. Now is our chance."

William recognized the voice immediately. The man had arrived with the first group of refugees and he complained constantly. He had finally hired on with one of the inns in the village and spent his days mucking out stables.

"We don't go anywhere until Scar Face arrives." The others stated again.

William figured he had heard enough. He drifted back down the long line slowly until he was standing next to Fredrick. When none of the other men seemed to be paying attention he spoke.

"Fredrick, it's me," William hissed so softly that only the other man could hear him.

"Yes, I spotted you when you came over the wall," Fredrick replied speaking out of the side of his mouth. "You should go warn your mother and the people of Villada."

William had not heard the name of the village surrounding the manor in such a long time he stopped momentarily and searched his mind.

"What about you?" William demanded. He was worried that if he left the old archer alone the men might kill him.

"I am an old warrior, William," Fredrick said with a soft smile that left as fast it came. "If there was one thing the crusade taught me it was how to survive."

Another skill that William thought it would be well worth learning, Fredrick seemed so calm and sure of the future. This was something William thought he could only gain if he carried through with his plan and joined the crusade.

"I will be back for you," William said. He drifted back along the line stopping to listen to conversations and even added a word of his own now and then. When he was twenty feet past the last bandit and he thought no one was looking, he hopped over the wall and headed out into the field under the cover of the darkness. The moon was only a sliver of its normal glorious self. The clouds were racing across the sky and William was able to stick to the shadows until he was across the field and onto a small trail that would lead him to the Villada.

He ran off into the night using his memory to guide him along a path that he had walked a thousand times throughout his early years.

It took him about ten minutes to reach the edge of the village and he sprinted along the quiet streets as the ache in his side grew. Finally, with his legs trembling he entered the small gate house and waved to the surprised sentry.

"Master William, where have you been, your mother has been worried sick after you," the sentry asked as he hurried to where William was struggling to regain his breath.

"Bandits are coming tonight," William sputtered as he accepted the cup of water and downed it in tree gulps.

"What!" the sentry exclaimed.

The man's name finally returned to William and he continued, "Adroal, go get my brother and roust the men still here. We need to warn the village and prepare them."

Adroal nodded and ran for the barracks next to the Manor. The building had been built in the last year to accommodate the growing number of soldiers Duke Edward was forced to employ to guard his estate.

William stood back to his feet and trotted towards the manor happy that his strength was returning quickly. He opened the door and saw the figure of his brother sitting at the long table.

"Conrad, thank the Savior you're awake yet," William burst out. "We need to get…"

"Where have you been!" Conrad nearly shouted.

"What?" William replied. "I went to Fredrick's to get the bows. But that is not important right now."

"Oh, what is important, your own laziness?" Conrad replied harshly. "What, did you find a spot to sleep or did you decide to spend the day exploring somewhere. Mom has been worried sick."

"Look!" William shouted back. "Bandits are less then a league from the manor and they know dad is not here! We can have to prepare."

"Likely story to cover your own laziness," Conrad sneered. He pointed to William's filthy clothes. "You look like you have been rolling in the mud."

"I don't have time for this," William said as he turned to go. "I am going to go warn the village and organize our defense. If you want to join us you may, if not… I don't care."

William turned and stomped out the door fuming. Every time his father left, Conrad was the same way. Lording over him the fact that he had been left in charge and not William. When he exited the manor, the score of soldiers still stationed at the manor were rushing out of the barracks and strapping on the weapons and shields. Adroal was directing them.

"This is it?" William asked. Aghast, he

knew that a large number of men had gone with his father but normally there would have been at least fifty stationed inside the manor and the village.

"Bring as many bows as you can carry," William ordered Adroal. "We are going to have to arm the villagers."

"Is that wise, sire?" Adroal asked.

"We have no choice," William replied. "There were at least two score bandits in the first group and there was a second group meeting up with them. I don't know how many more were coming."

They all grabbed six or eight bows and enough quivers to pass out with the bows and rushed out the gate down to the village.

"Round up as many men as you can and tell everyone else to lock their doors and hide," William ordered. "And send someone you trust out as a look out. We need some warning." There was an idea beginning in his mind but he needed to find enough men to carry it off. And he needed to pray to the Savior that the men they found could shoot straight enough to make it work. *Or* he thought, we need to draw them in really close.

Scar Face pulled his mount to a halt and looked about. Scattered around the intersection of the two wagon trails were forty of his men. He knew that the priest would not be happy with what he planned but he didn't care. He had spent years raiding the smaller villages around the Hardarva Wall until that single day when a Duke interrupted his plans.

"What is High Priest Gregor going to say?"

Scar Face looked back at the man who had dared to question his plan and frowned, immediately the man raised his hands and stepped back.

"What do we care of the ambitions of priests and kings," Scar Face snarled to the men around him. He was leading a second group of almost sixty men, bringing the group around him to almost a hundred.

"We have spent years in the Wilds, while those inside the borders of Britoria grow fat off the land." Scar Face continued. "Why should we work for what we want? That is not the way of the Wilds, the strong prey on the weak. That is how things should be. We deserve what we are about to take and I am not going to let any priest tell me different."

The men around him muttered their agreement. Many of them pulled their weapons out and smiled anxiously.

"Now we are going to march into the village and secure it," Scar Face ordered. "I want everyone rounded up and put in the center of the village. When the manor is looted and burned to the ground, we will take what we can carry and fire the village."

"What if they fight?" someone asked.

"Then we kill them," Scar Face said angrily. "Any more stupid questions?"

No one dared say anything else as his fist closed anxiously on his sword.

Scar Face pulled his mount around and motioned for the twenty or so riders to follow him. When they were all bunched at the head of the men on foot, he led them south towards the village.

"Light the torches," Scar Face ordered. "Let them know fear, let them know that they are not safe anywhere."

Within minutes one hundred torches were lit and burning brightly, filling the night with angry red flames. The road they were riding on looped around to the south side of the village and pierced directly through the center of the collection of cottages and shops. There was a big green area in the center of the village with a marble fountain and it erupted in three lines of water that rose about four feet into the air before crashing back to the pools below. When Scar Face reached the edge of the village he reined his mount to the side and let the flowing mass of his men pass by him. Most of his mounted soldiers followed suit.

"Anxious as I am to have my revenge I am not a fool," Scar Face said to his second in command. He was a hulking man mounted on an even bigger plow horse. Fruhaus stood over six and a half feet tall and weighed close to four hundred pounds.

"Anything you say, Scar," Fruhaus replied with a grin. A massive battle ax shifted in the harness on his back and seemed small when compared to his frame.

When the bulk of his men were past Scar Face pushed his mount along the village road. New cottages on each side spoke of wealth to him. When they reached the village square, Scar Face looked up to find the road entered an older section of the village and the dwellings and shops rose two stories into the air.

Curious he saw as he rode by the first set of buildings that something was blocking the area between the two structures. The same was true of the next set of buildings and suddenly he motioned to Fruhaus to stop.

"What is it Scar?"

"Something is wrong." He looked ahead and suddenly a great wagon used to move goods from the field to the storage bins rolled out from the side and crashed into a wagon sitting in the middle of the street. A second later it roared into flames and his men began to push back as they shielded their faces.

Then a second and third wagon rolled out and soon the street was blocked with a roaring blaze.

"Throw down your weapons!"

The bandits heard the shout from above them and looked up to see the youngest son of the Duke standing atop a crate near the burning wagons just to their right.

"Come down here and get them!" Most shouted back and jeered at him.

Suddenly the tops of the buildings around them were filled with the grim faces of villagers holding bows. Many were so scared their hands shook but a few narrowed their eyes in anticipation.

"Get them!" Scar Face shouted. He pulled his own bow from the back of his mount and loosed an arrow that struck a villager in the leg. With a cry of pain the man disappeared over the back of the roofline. Then the air was filled with shafts as his men tried to fire at the dim figures atop the buildings. From atop their perches high in the air the villagers and the few soldiers who were scattered among them rained arrows down on the bandits.

"Get back," Scar Face motioned his twenty or so riders that still hung back with him. As one they rode back down the alley

11 – Bandits Attack

William watched as the un-organized group of bandits moved up the road away from the village square and into the area they had hastily prepared.

"Get ready," William hissed at the men standing behind the big wagon. "Now!"

There was a groan of wooden wheels as the wagon creaked forward directed by a dozen strong backs, and rolled into the path of the bandits and came to a halt against the parked wagon. They had filled the first wagon with barrels of water and big pieces of timber until it formed a perfect barrier. The rolling wagon was doused in oil and the moment it stopped moving he tossed a torch into the soaked timbers.

"Get back," William shouted as he let the torch fly. Immediately the flames caught in the oil-soaked wood and he leapt back shielding his face from the inferno. When the path was mostly blocked, an eerie silence filled the road as the bandits tried to push back against their fellows who were still crowding the street.

"Throw down your weapons and you will be spared," William shouted loudly. He ducked as a crude spear arched out from the group before him and dug into the wood next to him. He drew back his bow and focused through the flames at the closest bandit. Suddenly, time seemed to slow down for him and the street faded from view until all he could see was the face of the man. Then he released his grip on the bow string and heard the twang as the arrow erupted from the end of the bow.

"Good shot, sire!"

William heard someone shout at him but all he saw was the surprised look on the bandits face as the arrow suddenly erupted from his chest. The man's hands closed around the shaft and a pained look filled his eyes. He clutched at it and then slipped to the ground. All around him a score of his fellows fell to the ground as the villagers released their arrows.

"Get down, sire!"

William was suddenly shoved to the ground as the bandits rushed to get around the barricade. Arrows rained down from atop the buildings and slowed some, but not all.

William pulled another arrow and spotted a bandit about to shoot one of his men in the back as he was engaged in a fierce sword fight. Without thinking he drew and released his arrow. It struck the man in the shoulder and the bandit's arrow went wild.

There was a sound of breaking glass and beyond the burning wagon William saw the attackers leaping into buildings and disappearing into the darkness. Even worse he saw the bandit leader with his horribly scarred face pull his mount around and lead at least twenty more mounted men into one of the side streets.

"Get up into the rooftops," William shouted at the twenty men who were with him on the ground. He leapt to his feet and ran as fast as he could to the sturdy steps that would lead him to the roof.

Once there he drew his bow and looked back, at the bottom of the stairs a man with filthy armor was starting up.

"Bad idea," William muttered as he sighted down the shaft and released it. The surprised face vanished but five more replaced it and William rolled away from the steps as two arrows dug deep grooves in the wood at his feet.

"They are coming up the steps!" William shouted to the seven men who were aiming their bows at various targets below them. Thankfully, two of his father's soldiers were there and they directed the villagers towards the stairs.

There was a rush of steps as the bandits swelled over the edge of the roof and an answering swoosh of seven bows as the three bandits were struck several times and thrown backwards off the steps. Then four more were atop the steps and William was forced to pull out his sword.

Clang

William threw up his sword just in time to catch the strike of a man who was missing most of his front teeth.

"Time to die, brat," the bandit snarled.

"I would rather not," William said as he intercepted the second blow and backed up a step. The man was stronger then he was but William knew he was faster. He struck fast and hard but his opponent turned away the attack. Back and forth they fought for what seemed like forever and suddenly William fell back over the body of one of the villagers. The bandit leapt over the top of him with a triumphant shout. William's sword skittered away but his hand fell on something sharp and he grabbed it and stabbed out.

There was a grim satisfaction as the bandit fell away with a wound on his stomach and turned to flee, his will to fight gone. Around him the rooftop was silent and William looked around. Five of his men had survived but two of the untrained villagers were moaning weakly on the timbers.

"They will survive, sire but they can't fight anymore."

William nodded, "Get them up to the manor." He sheathed his sword and grabbed his bow and fallen quiver. "The rest of you come with me." A quick glance around told him that the fighting had broken up into small groups and even though they had ambushed the bandits, there was still fight left in the men.

What worried William most was the disappearance of Scar Face and what trouble he could still cause. The three of them headed down into the street and immediately came across a pair of bandits about to finish off one of the soldiers from the manor.

William's arrow caught one of the bandits just below the arm and he knew without a doubt that the man was dead as he slipped to the ground.

"I yield!" cried the second bandit. He dropped his sword and raised his hands.

That was the turning point for the battle. William led his small group through the street sweeping up the villagers and changing the tide in battle after battle. Sometimes he arrived too late to help the innocent. When he arrived at the village green he skidded to a halt. Behind him there was a swelling group of nearly fifty villagers and the surviving twelve soldiers. Across the village William saw one of his men fall to Scar Face and he growled angrily.

He pulled back his bow and launched an arrow but just before the shaft took the bandit leader, he turned and the arrow struck down the man behind him.

"Enjoy your victory, boy," Scar Face shouted. "This is not over yet." The bandit pulled his horse about and led the nine men of his band that had survived out of the village at a gallop and moments later they had vanished into the night. Behind them they left a village in shambles.

"How many did we lose?" William asked later as he walked the street. Despite the battle casualties he felt excited and invigorated.

"Seven of your father soldiers died and almost thirty villagers." One of the men replied. "Only seventeen of the bandits surrendered, twenty-eight were killed, the rest fled."

"Find a place for the prisoners and my father can deal with them when he returns," William said. He was standing before the burned out remains of the wagons as a few villagers doused the embers with buckets of water.

"What of Scar Face?"

William shook his head. Suddenly he realized that he had completely forgotten about Fredrick and he slapped his face with his hand.

"Fredrick!" William burst out. "I hope he is alright." Two of the soldiers were nearby and William motioned for them to come over. "Gather up anyone who can ride, we need to search the fields to the north."

"What are we looking for?" one of the men asked as others rushed to gather up torches and lanterns.

"Not what," William said. "Who, Fredrick is out there somewhere."

Many of the villagers knew of the Freglander who crafted such fine bows and sold his extra spices at the market. Soon almost fifty men were armed with torches and bows and they spread out as they moved north from the village.

William anchored the center of the line as it swept around the short stone walls and drifted in and out of small stands of oaks. He was beginning to despair finding the old fletcher alive when suddenly there was an eruption of noise to his right.

"We found him, sir," men yelled.

William ran towards the noise and when he arrived was greeted with the sight of the old white-haired man. He was bound hand and foot to a thick tree trunk and there was a bit of cloth pressed into his mouth that kept him from crying out.

"Cut him down quickly," William said. When Fredrick was freed, William gave him a great hug and patted him on the back.

"It is good to see you again, boy," Fredrick said with a smile. He moved about carefully while the feeling returned to his limbs.

After gathering everyone back together William led them back to the Manor and posted a watch around the village. His brother had not been seen for most of the night but when William finally entered the manor, he saw the lone figure sitting before the fire. Steadfastly he ignored Conrad and walked wearily up to where his bed waited for him. Sleep came immediately and the next morning he did not awaken until the sun was high in the sky.

12 – *William's Demand*

Four months passed since the bandits attacked the village and the tense relationship between Conrad and William only grew worse. Duke Edward praised his youngest son when he returned and once again they all went about helping to rebuild lives lost during the fighting.

"Nonsense," Duke Edward said to Fredrick when the old fletcher said he was moving back to his burned out cottage. "You will stay here with us where you can be safe. A place will be arranged outside the village for your gardens."

Nothing was seen of Scar Face after that night but the thought that the bandit leader was still lurking in the Wilds made many people nervous.

It was two days before William's eighteenth birthday and he was sitting with Clair. The two of them were looking down at the small fishing stream where Charles had loved to sit and watch the fish. It was a beautiful sunny day and the grass was a vibrant green while the sky overhead was clear and a rich shade of blue. The stones of the bridge were warm from the sun and William leaned back with a contented sigh.

"When are you going to tell your father?" Clair asked sadly.

"Soon," William replied. "The army is marching in a few months and I want to be in time to get to the City of the King."

"Why must you go?" Clair asked again.

"I don't know," William replied. "I just know that I can't stay here with Conrad around."

They held hands for almost an hour and finally Clair rose to her feet. She looked down at William with her great blue eyes and asked him one last time.

"Don't do it, please," Clair said quietly.

"I have to," William replied with a shrug.

"When will I see you again?" Clair asked finally when she realized his mind was made up.

"I don't know," William replied. "It could be years."

"Goodbye," Clair said as tears filled her eyes. She turned and walked quickly away from him and back towards her father's manor.

William rose to his feet and turned to the north where his own home sat waiting for him. He walked slowly, enjoying the warmth of the day, and when he finally entered the village all was quiet. It was the end of the day and many in the small collection of houses were sitting down to their evening meal.

"Ah son, there you are," Duke Edward said.

William looked up at his father and saw the sadness in his eyes as though his father knew exactly what was coming.

"Father," William started. "I need to talk to you."

"What is it son?" Duke Edward asked

slowly He folded his hands over the leather bound scriptures before him and waited for his son to continue.

"I want my portion of the estate," William stated boldly. "I have decided to join the crusade."

There was a gasp from William's mother and Conrad and both began to speak at once. They both stopped when Duke Edward motioned for silence.

"You know what you are asking for, Son?" Duke Edward asked him with a raised eyebrow. "This war they are about to begin is not just."

"It is what I wish to do, Father," William replied. "I have been thinking about this for six months and not once has my mind wavered. I want my portion of the inheritance and I will give up any claims I have to this land or titles forever."

William saw the greed erupt in Conrad's eyes as he made his offer and he wished he could point it out to his father. Instead his father nodded and motioned for them both to follow him.

"William?"

He turned to where his mother was crying freely now and tears misted his eyes.

"I am sorry, mum," William said to her as he embraced her closely. "This is something that I must do."

Duke Edward led Conrad and William into the little used back room of the manor and motioned for them both to be seated. There was a thick strong box bolted to the floor and a small desk with a thick book on it. The room smelled of ink and several quills were laid out in perfect order on the desk.

"This is our family's records," Duke Edward said to his sons. "It catalogues what we own and what it is worth. As the younger son William, your portion is one third of all I possess.

William emerged from the manor the next day with a letter of introduction to the king and a small strong box filled with gold coins. His father had given him enough coins to cover one third of all he owned.

"You are always welcome back here anytime, Son."

William thought about his father's words but the excitement of the day was too much for him to even consider when he would return to the manor, if he ever decided to return. He hugged his mother for a long time and shook hands with his father. Conrad was absent when he left-that suited William fine.

"What's this?" William asked as Bernard hoisted a thick pack and motioned for him to lead the way.

"I am going with you, boy," Bernard said with a shake of his head. "It may be that I can keep you from getting killed."

William smiled and shook Bernard's hand vigorously. His day was brightening with each step.

He did not see Clair as he walked down the wide wagon road that would bring him to the Hardarva Wall and into Britoria. That fact made him a bit sadder but soon he was smiling again.

The day was perfect with a warm sun shining down on him and Bernard as they walked leading their pack horse and in William's opinion the future was bright.

The End

Coming Soon

Journey of the Prodigal Son.

MATTHEW J KRENGEL

*Matthew lives in the Sauk Rapids area of Minnesota with his family. He is an avid reader and writer and loves fantasy. After growing up in central Minnesota and attending college at Pensacola Christian College he moved back to Minnesota and began writing. His first book **Staff of Elements** was published in 2011 and he has a young adult fantasy **The Map Maker** being released by NorthStar Press in September of 2012. He is busy preparing several self published books and hopes someday to make writing his full time occupation. Visit his website at www.mjkbooks.com for regular updates.*

Made in the USA
Charleston, SC
26 December 2012